Remains Of Me

Remains Of Me

Abhilasha Gupta

Edited By Khushi Arora

Copyright © 2020 Abhilasha Gupta

All rights reserved. No part of this book may be reproduced, stored, or transmitted by any means-whether auditory, graphical, mechanical, or electronic-without written permission of the author. Any unauthorized reproduction of any part of this book is illegal and is punishable by law.

To the maximum extent permitted by law, the author and publisher disclaim all responsibility and liability to any person, arising directly or indirectly from any person taking or not taking action based on the information available in this publication.

ISBN 13: 978-93-90507-16-0
ISBN 10: 93-90507-16-2

Printed in India and published by BUUKS.

DEDICATIONS

This book is dedicated to my parents:

My mother: The purest soul I've ever come across.
My father: A role model and an unbelievably flawless human being.
Thank you for making me a fragment of you, for inspiring me every day and for giving meaning to everything I do. You have made all my dreams come true.

To Rivansh, I hope you grow up to read this and learn what bo believed in. Hope someday this inspires you. Thanks for changing my life.

TABLE OF CONTENTS

Gratitude	ix
The Last Night in America	1
Hello India!	9
Midnight Stranger	13
Jay and I	23
An Uber And A Nerd	30
Happy Birthday, Jay	35
Auto Pilot	43
What Sisters Do	51
Revelation And Realization	55
What I Call Home	61
Déjà vu	68
It Started With A Break-Up	72
Only The Blind Can Love	75
Inaya	80
An Incorrigible Flirt	85
The Twisted Dream I	88
The Twisted Dream II	97
The Reason Is You	106

Crossing Oceans	110
Forrest	116
Black As Sin	120
Crusading	126
Losing hope	132
We'll be fine	138
Epilogue	145

GRATITUDE

Thanks to my family, Sarthak and Ayushi for constantly giving me reasons to take the leap.

Special thanks to Vishal for being the greatest critique in the world. I hope this final copy suffices at least.

Ken and Simran- seriously, thanks for putting up with me and making my day everyday. Cheers

You, the one reading this book: Thanks for being a part of my journey. Welcome to my first book.

Also, a very heartfelt thanks to everyone I have ever crossed paths with. Everything has led to this today, thanks for being a part of my story.

THE LAST NIGHT IN AMERICA

I sat at one of the loneliest beaches in California, with a cigarette in my hand, watching the settling nightfall. I loved sunsets. I saw them as the drowning of today's misery and the promise of a new tomorrow. I cherished the coarse yet tender sand which embraced my toes with a soft touch that I wasn't used to; the ocean told me tales of its crusade through the waves crashing onto the shore right before me. I wondered about the creatures in the ocean; a different, peaceful world that existed right underneath our chaos. And us? We just saw their world as a realm to tour and a business to run. But it wasn't our fault. Most of us are trained to perceive everything as an escape or a money-making establishment.

"What are you thinking?" Alec gazed at me, with an affection that was alien to me. I had met him at the university. He was a simple Scottish-American guy, who could magically make me feel secure even when I was at my vulnerable worst. While he was here, settling my sanity, I was getting over his best friend and former roommate, Abrar.

"Look at this ocean, Alec," I took a long, dramatic pause. "I was thinking how could God create something as beautiful as this and something so ugly as you at the same time?"

Deflection has always been my strong point.

"Oh boy! I like it when you're quiet," he said as we both broke into light laughter.

"You know, I read somewhere that a world of silence is a vast fullness. I see it now," I said as I started filling my fist with the sand. The tighter I held on to it, the quicker it slipped away. That was exactly how I was failing to keep myself together in my current situation.

"Let's get out of here, Ally. They just posted a check-in nearby on Facebook; I don't want to run into them," Alec said as he started packing up our stuff in his extraordinarily large backpack.

Yes, Alec and I had an undercover friendship. He was extra careful to never let his friends know that he was hanging out with me. I hoped that he wasn't embarrassed by me, knowing that his friends were not fond of me, crediting a big part to their guilt. Maybe they disliked me because I took a stand against their guy, Abrar. Maybe they were too scared of him. Alec used to believe it was the latter. I didn't trust him because I wasn't petrified of Abrar, he was just a tiger who needed to be tamed, or more like a feisty dog.

Alec and I often took trips across the West Coast so I could get over *The Situation*. We never waited for the weekend. One moment, we'd be sitting playing video games on a wednesday afternoon and the next thing you know, we'd be packing our bags and driving off to Los Angeles. Not surprisingly, even tonight we picked up some snacks and lots of beer, put on our favorite music, and drove off to Lytle Creek in our convertible. It was my spot.

Like any other night, it was past 1 AM and pitch dark. We could hear the coyotes howl but that was common in San Bernardino. I sat next to him behind the Bonita Falls, as the melodies of the falling water and the murmur of the bugs filled my heart to plenty. I reached inside my leather jacket and pulled out a black necklace. I had bought the necklace at Westminster Abbey as a symbol of hope a few years ago. It had a little peace sign on it.

As I stared at the necklace and rubbed it goodbye, I put it towards Alec.

"It's my last night here buddy. I want you to keep this because I might never see you again. I want you to remember me and our time here through this necklace, for eternity," I said as I enveloped his arm into mine.

"Come on, Ally. Be realistic! Your witty self is unforgettable." He nuzzled my shoulder in return.

"Okay, can I do the talking now? I've spent months, hiding what I feel from everyone. I just can't go back and regret not telling you what you deserve to know." I realized how bad I was at gestures as I started rubbing a pebble nervously.

Alec nodded with a smirk as if he knew what was coming.

"You saved me. You kept me whole and had my back through something I never thought I'd face. You led me on my road to recovery and took me places. You made me feel safe when I was the most vulnerable. While I am uncertain why you did all this for me, I don't know how I will ever reciprocate. I am thankful, Alec, forever," I said as I looked down and away from his eyes in gratitude.

Unwittingly so, I broke down in front of him for the first time.

"Ally, come on. Stop saying all of this. This is what friends are for." He gave me a side hug. "You have seen enough and I can't see you like this. You should go back, away from all this. Let me come with you to the airport tomorrow. Please!" Alec insisted like a child as he tied the necklace around his wrist.

"Nah, that's too much. I have driven around too much with you. I wanna make the most of my time left here by hitting on a random cabbie now." We cracked up. "I'll be fine. Don't worry."

We stood up, lit our cigarettes, and stared at the flowing water, saying nothing. As the mist from the falling water touched our skin softly, Alec turned towards me and we hugged our time out. Everything flashed before my eyes. This was one of our closest moments together. All we could hear was the falling water and each other's heartbeats.

I kept thinking - this is it. This was the end of our journey in America. We toasted to the moment as we made our way to McDonald's to help our screeching stomachs.

As we waited for the food in the drive-thru, I kept switching songs on the radio. I was hungry and hence, annoyed. Alec could see my face frying up. I blamed it on the empty thoughts. "Ally, I know you're not okay with leaving mid-semester. It's okay. We have to do stuff like that for our family sometimes." Alec stared at my frowning face.

"I think I'm just hungry."

"When will you start talking about the real stuff, Alisha? I thought we were close enough."

Before he could continue, I decided to change the subject. The odds turned into my favour when a black sports car passed by. It looked like a freaking batmobile. We shamelessly drooled over the car. Especially me.

"What on earth is this thing?" Alec looked startled.

"The Bugatti Veyron Super Sport. I present to you the fastest car in the world, Alec." My eyes widened. "It goes 267 mph."

"There you go, my little car nerd. Is there any car you don't know about?" My sick knowledge of cars always startled Alec.

I felt a little insulted since that car got its food instantly. Seriously McDonald's? You're forgiven, though. It's a freaking BVS!

The car took off, quite literally sounding like an aeroplane taking off. "0 to 60 in 2.4 seconds," I said in utter awe. A waitress from inside walked up to us. She was staring at the car too. She handed us our food and still proud of our Dodge, we headed back to the university village in the dying night.

I was a student at Cal State University and it was our last semester. I was leaving early because I had to attend a wedding. My sister had graduated recently and thus, decided to get married to her long term boyfriend. The prep for this grand Indian wedding would take at least a month. I had managed to get an early release due to my good grades. At least, that was what I was supposed to believe. However, I knew it was mostly because of my wealthy father. He could get anything done.

I hurriedly packed all my stuff without a single thought. At that point in my life, I had decided to accept whatever was going to come my way. The lesser I thought, the better it was. So I chose to live a simple life with a certain denial which made me feel freer.

Just then, my phone rang. It was my ex-boyfriend and current friend Abheer, face timing me. It had been a while since we had broken up. Familiarity had led us to a certain understanding which made me excuse his complications sometimes. He also reminded me of home, which I had begun to miss.

"Hey, Abheer. I am packing. What do you want?" I said in an annoying tone as I hurriedly packed my things into huge bags.

"I wanna see you when you come back. We are going to chill." He hinted inverted commas with his fingers at the word chill. I knew what he meant.

I stared at him in disgust. "Abheer, look. We all use hand gestures to express ourselves from time to time and some have a stronger place in our daily communication than others, but you and your inverted commas can literally lick a cactus." I had no tolerance for his bullshit anymore.

"You can't talk to me like that," he said in his usual high headed tone.

"I can do whatever I want, hon." I hung up.

This was progress, I thought to myself. I was standing up for myself and learning to say no. Kudos, Alisha! I had finally taken a stand for my choices. I also felt guilty, because no matter how bad our break up had been, I still felt a million things for Abheer. I continued stuffing my bags with all the shopping I had done in the name of "retail therapy" over the last few months.

While all my thoughts were finding insipid ways to circle inside me, I witnessed the beautiful Californian sunrise. All my classmates at college were getting ready for their classes while I was getting ready to leave it all behind. I was excited to go home but it was all too bittersweet for me not to get overwhelmed.

Alec came to wake me up but instead, found me dressed and ready to go. We made our way to the RA's room and sorted out my dues and release. After having donated most of my stuff to the student's union, I headed out to the cafeteria to get a sandwich because even after all these years, I did not trust airport food. Walking to the cafeteria, I was surrounded by goodbyes.

Cal State's Subway counter was always empty. Students preferred burgers and stir fry instead. Patricia, the subway lady, had been serving the same sandwich to me for the last one year. I was super choosy with my food.

"Here's The Alisha Special." She ran out of the counter to hug me.

"Aww! You're the best, Patricia. I'll miss your sandwiches in India." I looked straight into her eyes and gave her an awkward hug. Inside me, there wasn't the slightest trace of any attachment whatsoever.

"I threw in extra chicken," she whispered in my ears, smiling through her emotions.

These people were sweet, emotional and expressive, and I was fond of them. It was probably my built-up insecurity since no one had ever really expressed their feelings to me.

When I reached my dorm, an old classmate Niya and a few other friends were standing in front of me. She had known me for a long time. "Guys, come on! I haven't spoken to y'all in months. This is so unexpected!" I was overwhelmed.

"Well yeah, screw you for that, bitch, but you are leaving now...so we had to be here!" Niya said with a bright smile as she reached out to hug me.

Another awkward hug.

I had my sandwich; I had my goodbyes. Now, I had to accept the fact that it was my time to go. I loaded the cab with my luggage and prepared for the final farewell.

As I looked at Alec, one last time, my eyes desperately searched for Inaya. My best friend Inaya. "I'll take care of her, believe me," Alec whispered.

HELLO INDIA!

I had a connecting flight from Los Angeles to New Delhi via London. It was 23 hours of travel. I had 23 hours to think and settle myself into what had happened and make peace with it.

I kept pondering over a quote by Rumi :

'*The moment you accept what troubles you've been given, the door will open.*'

Throughout the drive, my heart kept pounding. I was leaving so much here. I was leaving behind the girl that I never knew I could be. Was I leaving her behind or taking her with me? A thousand thoughts circled my mind.

"You got this. You'll be yourself again once you're there, they'll understand," I repeated to myself as I entered the LAX. In the last few months, I had learned to hype myself up like that to prepare for situations I was scared to face. Thorned by multiple people over time, I had become my very own cheerleader.

With a saturated mind, I cleared security and checked in. My subconscious was still not ready to let Alec fade into the back of my head. This was the first time I was without him in America. Ughh, I was going to miss that pig.

As soon as I boarded the plane and buckled up, I felt free; free from all the menace that had started to surround my life; free from the pressure of being accepted or understood. But all those people were history now. I started to reassure myself that I was going back to my family. I was going to forget all of it because I was going home.

All these thoughts had drained my energy and I felt exhausted. I just couldn't stop thinking.

My reverie was interrupted when an old man and a kid walked up to me. He tossed his stuff on the seat next to me while checking me out. I was sulking in my seat and probably making him wonder what was wrong with me. "Hey," he said, smiling wide while the kid looked at me with puppy eyes.

"Hi," I smiled back, trying very hard to keep it real.

"You're travelling alone?"

I looked at him wondering how it mattered to him. I was already so tired; I had no patience for a chit chat.

"My grandson here has never flown before. Why don't you let him take your window seat?" He said in a commanding tone while he picked his grandson's stuff and started keeping it in the net-pouch against the seat in front of me without even hearing my answer.

"Excuse me. I did not say yes!" I said harshly, taking his stuff out of the net-pouch. "I am going to sit in the seat I reserved 8 hours before this flight. You can't call in at the end and sit wherever you want to!" My first public outburst was a result of the fear of losing what's mine. He was alarmed and people were staring at me. I could not have cared less. I got comfortable in my seat and looked outside my well-earned window. It was the first time I had ever fought for myself.

In a matter of a few minutes, I fell asleep. Have you ever fallen asleep during a takeoff? This was a first for me. It was 10 hours of deep sleep till London when a crew member woke me up. I had not slept for such a stretch in a year.

A blonde English woman dressed in the tightest skirt and shirt I knew and a funny hat with American Airlines written on it, poked me multiple times in the shoulder to wake me up. I could feel the old man judging me for taking the window seat and then keeping it closed by falling asleep the whole way. I didn't blame him.

We were in London. I could tell by the clouds. My food table was filled with packed airline food. I gorged on the brownies and a sandwich and hurriedly stuffed the rest of it in my handbag. I slept in America and woke up in London. I felt like a depressed psychopath.

Next up was a 5-hour-long lay off at Heathrow. I spoke to Alec the whole time which mostly consisted of me complaining about the busiest airport in the world not having a single Subway sandwich.

Finally, I boarded the flight straight to my heart - New Delhi. I slept again. I woke up somewhere above Kazakhstan, shocked because I was anything but a sleeper. Was I trying to escape reality? I asked myself. Was I too scared to talk about it? Or way too immersed in it?

I went to the lavatory. I had not taken a wee in 21 hours. I looked at myself in the mirror and cried. I cried for no reason.

"Listen to me, Alisha. You are not taking any of these memories back with you. Akira is getting married and your major focus should be her. What happened with you should be buried deep inside. You cannot let it overpower you. Get your shit together, dammit!" I promised myself, looking at my tear-strewn face in the mirror. I felt angst inside me, I was furious, everything came flashing right before my eyes. In dire need of escape, I smacked my face hard. At that very moment, I stepped out of my thoughts.

Get your shit together, for Akira. This was not my first time putting my sister's feelings ahead of mine. I washed my face and pulled my hair down, just the way my dad liked it.

We had reached New Delhi earlier than scheduled, so the pilot was taking us over the city in circles until the air traffic control permitted him to land. I could look at all those places my dad used to take me as a kid. Qutub Minar, The Red Fort, The India Gate, I could see it all. I was trying to recognize these places from 20,000 feet. I had not felt this nostalgic before.

As the plane got closer to the ground, another unanticipated thought came to my fore. My father had never raised his voice to me. He had always treated me like a feather. How would I tell him that his daughter who had gone away for a year was now coming back all bruised and abused? He'd be shattered.

One step at a time, Alisha. I closed my eyes, clenched my fists, and forced myself to bury these thoughts inside.

Finally, I reached New Delhi with a dollop of anxiety mixed with excitement. My family – Mom, Dad, and Akira – were waiting for me. As soon as I saw them, I forgot everything. I was home and I was safe. Abrar was oceans away, but Inaya's face continued to flash before my eyes.

MIDNIGHT STRANGER

"Alisha, it's been a week since you returned from California! You can't be jet-lagged still. Wake up or I know a thousand ways to get you out of bed!" My mom's voice bellowed as I cocooned myself in the bed through the afternoon.

This was my escape. I was constantly tired, grumpy, and hungry. I had been curled up in this giant bed ever since I got back. Alec was the only person I was talking to because honestly, nobody had even cared to ask me why I had chambered myself in my room.

I was neither great nor famous. But I was human, which was the most complicated job in the world. At that point, I was not seeking any sympathy or courage; I was only expecting some acknowledgement. The only thing that seemed more complicated than that was being a part of a family which consisted of my self-made millionaire dad who was the biggest darling in the world, my mostly angry mum who loved me secretly, and my recently graduated and smitten sister.

In a week, I had made peace with the fact that no one was going to show interest in my changing behaviour. They would rather complain about it. I wished someone would ask me. I could feel my body change. I couldn't reckon if it was my changed lifestyle or Abrar's traces. I wanted to ask my mom if it was okay. Were chronic nausea and pelvic pain normal? Google scared me. Who could suggest if my irregular cycles signalled an underlying issue? I had a zillion stories to tell and even more questions to ask. I wished mom or Akira would walk in just once.

My parents were sensible. They had raised us to eat together and call each other every day when one or the other was away. In a sense, we were a protected, close-knit family. Unlike me, Akira was very open about her issues. Somehow, I thought that this exhausted my parents and left no space for me. Before I could have told my mom about Abrar, she had made it all about her issues with her soon-to-be mother-in-law. And I was used to this pettiness. During many of her breakdowns, she had also expressed her grief over my success. A success that didn't even exist yet.

"Ali slept all day again. She eats and sleeps. Is this why we spent our fortune on her education, so a potato in my fridge could be more productive than her?" Maa complained to dad as we ate, and everybody continued because nobody dared to mess with her. I knew where this was coming from. Akira's constant bickering had her bugged.

Dad gulped his food and said, "Alisha, this behaviour is unacceptable. Look at your sister, settling in life. You're not even trying to get a job. You know you're capable of good things. Your uncle had warned me about this. So you see sweetheart, I have to prove a lot of people wrong. Get up at 6 am tomorrow onwards and make something of yourself." Dad was just trying to keep up with mom.

Countless thoughts clouded my head. Since when did Maa keep her potatoes in the refrigerator? And why was waking up at 6 am a solution to every problem? Akira was settling because she had no career in the first place. If my family really cared, why hadn't they just asked me what was wrong instead of getting all worked up about how upset I was? How could I tell them I was not okay? How could I tell Akira that I was suicidal?

I nodded and decided to focus on the food. My sister wanted to take this chance and declare herself the responsible one like always.

"Papa, I know some people in the media industry. Even though I didn't get a chance to get degrees from top international universities, I can help Alisha build a career."

"Please. You only know some wedding photographers which are not the media industry, for heaven's sake. Stay out of my way, Akira." I burst.

"Alisha, behave yourself! She is older than you," my mom growled at me again. I could see the anger on my father's face.

There. I had disappointed them again. She was older and I was supposed to respect her even though her jealousy was clearly on the loose. In my family, I being the younger one was supposed to take the high road. For some reason, Akira was always right. The first born's feelings always mattered more. I liked to think all my frequent outbursts and insecurities were a result of Akira's behaviour but the reality was that she was the one who always needed extra attention. Always.

"I am sorry, Akira." I was peace-loving and I understood my parents would expect me to do this. They didn't want me to be hurt so they pretended to be okay with everything.

The whole tension in the air made it abundantly clear that no one was going to come and talk to me. As always, I would have to get out of my virtual grave on my own.

I finished my dinner and went for a walk in the garden. I had been apologising to Akira forever but every time I did that, it murdered my dignity. I only did it for the sake of my family.

My father walked up to me. "What are you thinking?" He asked. Dad knew how I felt but he was too scared to change things and hence, felt helpless.

I stopped near the seat bench and looked him in the eye. "Was I wrong, daddy?"

"Akira is getting married, Als. She is mature now, we need to treat her with respect."

"But didn't you see that *she* insulted me first? She always does that, papa."

"She has so many things going on. Her fiancé doesn't want the same venue as her. She is struggling, Alisha. She is not in the right space of mind right now. You must understand."

He better be kidding me right now. She was allowed to fall apart over this?

"Okay, papa. I'll take care of her. Sorry."

"You're my strongest soldier and I love you, pumpkin." He hugged me and his embrace made me forget everything.

I waited until after dinner and went to my room. It was the best time of the day. I could now do whatever I wanted, preferably even sob in the corner. I opened my Facebook as a pre-bed ritual when my constant scrolling was brought to a sudden halt. Abheer Singh is engaged! Goddamn engaged. He never told me and still wanted to "*chill*." Anger surged in me and my blood boiled to a point where it could've burst out any minute. What a lying piece of shit.

I needed to rant. I was angry at everyone. My family, Abheer, and the things Abrar had done had left me extra sensitive.

In dire need of escape, I started looking for someone to talk to. Alec must be at the uni and my other friends had already told me they were tired of me talking about Abheer. Where could I find someone new at 1 am?

Tinder! Inaya's favorite. It took me 2 minutes to register my profile and 3 minutes to get my first match. Jay Arora.

His profile was not very unique. It had 3 pictures of him where he looked different in each. He was a software developer, a TEDx speaker, and a hardcore nerd. I swiped right because he was a speaker. Oratory skills are attractive.

He instantly texted me.

Hey Alisha, I am Jay. You can google me to find out more.

This was followed by a link. Snob alert!

His comment credited to my already torched emotions. I hastily typed.

Hey Jay, I'd rather talk to you and get to know what google doesn't know about you.

He didn't reply to this for like 5 minutes. What a waste of time! I went back to swiping more people. After getting around 7 more matches, a reply popped up.

What do you want to know about a geek who can't really tell tales?

I wanted someone who could just listen anyway.

Well, for starters, is he interested in hearing me rant about a pathetic ex-boyfriend?

Sounds boring.

He responded without giving it a thought, triggering my insecurities at my most impulsive self.

Why don't you call me at +91 999998881 and find out if it's actually boring?

It was never my thing to give away my number like that, but crying in the night hunting for people to talk to was not me either. So, I guess they just crossed each other out.

7 minutes had passed and my frustration started shifting from Abheer to Jay. How could he not respond to a girl giving him her number? But he wasn't that interesting anyway. *Google me, my ass!* What a pathetic excuse for a human, I thought in exasperation.

The phone rang with an unknown number. Well, who else could it be?

I sat up and fixed my hair as if he was going to see me. For some weird reason, I even cleared my throat twice before answering.

I answered but didn't speak. There was silence on both ends. I wanted to hear his voice first. He finally spoke. "I had to wrap up all my work to call you, which I never ever do, so please start, miss."

That made me smile wide. What a nice voice. My mind started picturing him with that voice as he spoke. That became the thing about Jay. He could make me smile even in the most terrible situations.

"So, his name is Abheer and I dated him four years ago. We still talk and all and I just found out he has a girlfriend who he never told me about. Who does that? Why are guys like that?" My voice started to sharpen as the tirade went on.

"Why did he even come back to me if he was dating her? Goodness, do men not have a heart? He is the worst guy I've ever met. How can someone be so cruel? He needs to shift to another planet or something. I hate him," I blabbered on.

"You know he cheated on me with my friend, and then gaslighted me into thinking it was my fault. I am so done with men. I am never forgiving him. Are you even there? Hello?" My voice was met with dead silence.

Suddenly, an innocent laughter pealed on his end. "Why are you talking to him then?"

My words choked me for a few seconds because I didn't know the answer to his question. But come on, he was supposed to be favouring me instead of attacking me like this.

"Well, technically, now I'm not. He is a good friend. He broke up with me but then called after 6 months to rekindle our friendship. There is a bond which you'll not understand, of course, so don't judge me," I defended myself.

"Alisha, listen. It doesn't matter if I am judging you. What matters is that he's a jackass for cheating on you and I don't understand why you are so upset if he had a girlfriend the whole time. Do you think she knows he still talks to you? I don't think so." Jay had started to make sense.

"Once a cheater, always a cheater. She is never going to be happy with him and will eventually leave him. He is someone else's problem now. So, for what it's worth, you're better off without him. Why don't you focus on yourself rather than focusing on someone who is not meant to stay? Wise up!" He spoke with a tinge of surety in his voice.

I stopped my tirade and went silent again, though this time it was comfortable. It was like both of us were thinking something. Deep down, I had realized that I already knew everything Jay said. My frustration had nothing to do with Abheer. It was the aftershocks of the devastating destruction caused by Abrar, complemented by my family's unrealistic expectations which were oozing out on Abheer.

Breaking the silence. Jay said, "That story was boring, indeed. I knew it would be."

"Whatever," I rolled my eyes. A wasteful expression over a phone call added emotion.

"Do you want to play 20 questions? We both can ask each other questions and we will have to give honest answers."

"Oh, I do like questions," I said, thankful that he had changed the topic.

"Alright, so what's the craziest thing you've ever done?" Jay asked after thinking hard.

"Checking my psycho levels already?" I giggled.

"Trust me when it comes to the psycho meter, the more psychotic the girl, the better."

I was too overwhelmed to wonder where Jay had collected this data from and thus, indulge in any kind of logical reasoning.

"Well, I was in Vegas this summer and I lost all my money at the casino. So, I stripped at a bar for a free burger!" I narrated this story in the most shameful way possible, trying to test him.

Jay was shocked, "Damn girl! Now that is something. I was in Vegas too, for Hackathon. Crazy, had I been at that bar."

"Well, in that case, it would have been more than a burger for me." That was me. A barefaced flirt.

Silence. So much silence on the phone. I hated it.

"Hello? What happened? I was joking!" I enquired.

"Well, I usually don't know what to say in such situations. I get tongue-tied."

"I see. So my turn now? Why would you want to hear a random stranger rant about a failed relationship at 2 am on a Saturday?" I tucked myself flat on the bed bracing myself for a long story.

"Because I am a data collector. I'd like to see how you would talk about me once I break your heart."

"Ewww, that is the saddest joke ever," I exclaimed.

"Honestly? I am amazed by myself. I am an introverted workaholic, Alisha. I don't even call my best friends to hear their rants, don't know why I did this. But I do know one thing. I don't regret it. there's something different about you."

"You have spoken to me for like 10 minutes. How do you know I am different?"

"I think the rant had nothing to do with Abheer." He sounded confident.

"Fuck." I couldn't come up with anything else. Was this tinder geek a magician too?

"Okay, so do you think cereal is soup?" Jay came up with his best ice-breaker.

"What, no."

"Why not?"

"Wow, I don't know that." I couldn't think of an answer.

"If peanut butter was not called peanut butter, what would it be called?"

And before we knew it, the sun had risen and we had talked about everything - from our biggest fears to our favourite chocolates. We went on and on and I didn't want that night to end. While it was time for Jay to finish his work, I decided to impress my dad by waking up at six in the morning.

JAY AND I

Sometimes when you are in a dark place, you think you have been buried, but you've been planted - Christine Caine

I woke up smiling for a change, eyes open wide. I replayed Jay's voice in my head as I stretched my arms out. It was surreal. I was happy and dreamy; but deep down I knew I wasn't feeling this way for the first time. This always ended badly, always. I could hear my voice in my head shrieking *hell no!* as soon as I started thinking about my conversation with Jay. As I thought of his voice while brushing my teeth, my conscience slapped me in the face and I felt disappointed in myself.

It was so confusing. Was I supposed to be happy? I wasn't waking up tired and depressed or disappointed in creating another trap for myself. Is it always so messy being 23?

I checked my phone to see if Jay had texted. He had not. But my sister surely had. I rolled my eyes because I knew it wouldn't bring good news.

```
Alisha, wake up! You have to go meet Tina Aunty at
her office. She will help you with your job search.
```

Yeah right, Akira, a search that hadn't even started yet. I rolled my eyes again. This was the only way I was allowed to express my feelings for her without pissing her off. Why did she always think she could steer my life any way she wanted? I threw myself on the bed with bitter annoyance but like always, got up and rolled with the stones.

As I left my room in my pyjamas, mom looked at me with a twinkle in her eye. This was the most hopeful she had felt for me in a very long time. "Now, everything will be fine," she said, running her palm down my head.

I smiled through my frustration and flung myself onto the couch. I checked my phone again. Was Jay still asleep?

Tina Aunty was known for being a 'Big Shot' in our family. She was nothing more than a hamster on the corporate wheel, but my family believed earnestly that she would introduce me to her enormous network, helping me build my corporate career. I had three degrees and multiple certifications on my resume. My father had suggested several strengths and qualities, I could highlight on my resume, sanity not being one of them.

My mother fed me curd and jaggery before I left as it was known to bring good luck. Like any luck could help me feel stable or like a thousand mints could solve the problem my mother had just created in my mouth!

After two train journeys and two cab rides, I had finally reached her multi-storeyed office building. But oh boy, had I lost touch with the boiling summers of India. I had been facing issues with my health lately; due to all the travelling and wedding preps, I think. But ever since I had returned home, I had been as lazy as a sloth. By now, I should've slept over the dizziness and nausea which followed even the slightest exertion, but I guess my body just needed a hard push. With these thoughts in my mind, I walked into the professional haunts of Tina Aunty, pleasantly surprised.

That building was made of glass top to bottom. It looked like a mini version of The Shards, defying physics with hanging floors. I couldn't help but stare for a moment. "One day Ally, one day," I said to myself. I had always dreamt of being an entrepreneur and following in my father's footsteps. I wanted to build an office just like this. At that moment, I knew I could have given anything to die with memories and not dreams.

Wearing my tight dress and feeling slightly conscious of my stress fat, I entered the building. Passing four security checks and three registration counters, I finally reached her cabin.

At the front desk, I made acquaintance with a make-up clad, attractive girl who had a serious glance towered over me, making me feel like an imposter. I was told to wait because Tina Aunty was in a meeting. I took a seat and looked around for a bit. Conversations about discounted lunch menus and quitting cigarettes echoed in my ear as I found myself feeling weird. I had been cynical from the start but still expected a certain zeal for innovation and creativity in an office. This place was simply disappointing. A lavish building filled with slaves.

Tina Aunty's assistant asked, "Do you have an appointment?" I was startled by her high-pitched voice. I was cursing my sister at this moment because I knew she must have not scheduled this.

"I guess not, but she knows me, I am family. Could you tell her Alisha Mehra is here?" I said hesitatingly, conscious of the jaggery stuck in my teeth.

"Ma'am, family members are not really allowed in the official premises. Why don't you wait in the coffee lounge while

I pass on the message?" She looked at me like I had just committed a felony.

"Okay, sure, where to?" I asked her nervously as she ignorantly walked off in her high heels.

So, I led myself to the lounge after losing my way a few times and finally settled into overhearing more conversations. Everybody just looked sad. Not the kind of sad I was but an eerie permanent kind of troubled. They were all dressed in uniforms, white shirts and black bottoms. It almost seemed like the boredom on their faces was being exemplified in what they wore.

I poured myself two shots of espresso and sat in a corner. Everybody was so depressed there, I could really use a smoke. Aunt Tina finally entered the cafeteria, waving shamelessly at me.

"Alisha! Oh baby, when did you return? It is so good to see you!" Aunt Tina flung her arms wide open.

"It is great to see you too, Aunty! How have you been?" I said awkwardly hugging her.

"Oh, please call me Tina! By the way, what's with the accent?" Aunt Tina said judgingly.

"Accent, me? Uhh?" I was so confused as I bottomed my espresso. I double-checked my accent. Turned out it was Tina aunty's presumed notion.

"Anyway, I read your resume that Akira had sent me and I'll surely send it to some people I know."

"That would be a big help, Aunty. Thanks. The office looks great, by the way!" Lying was not my forte but I tried.

"I know right. It's a dream come true. Still can't believe a girl from the Mehra family is working at Y&E!" She claimed proudly.

"Yes, Aunty. We all look up to you." I was scared, in case she saw through my fake empathy. But she seemed too self-involved to care.

"So, did you meet any boys abroad? Any new guys I should be knowing off?" She poked me in the arm, getting eerier gradually.

"Umm, Aunty. Don't embarrass me now…" Tina Aunty was the one relative in the family who had a career but lacked the grace to carry it. I felt embarrassed and started coughing to avoid the topic.

"Yeah, maybe the Delhi air isn't suiting you anymore." She got weirder with each sentence and I was scared to hear what was coming next.

"Lost your V-V? Huh?" She winked with a grin.

"I don't know what it is aunty, I think I should be heading home." I started wrapping my things up consciously.

"Yeah yeah, secretive! Tell your new white boyfriend that Aunt Tina says hi," She giggled. My insides cringed to the core.

It was the only time I had ever sprinted out of a building. They were the creepiest 10 minutes of my week.

I left the building, lit a cigarette in the smoking-room and took a puff of relief. I vented out my frustration. I did not need this.

I looked at my phone. A text and a missed call. Both from Jay!

Hey, I slept so nice. Where you at? Did you sleep? Call me.

It was his first text message.

Within a second, I dialled his number. He answered. "Hey tinder girl, Good morning!" Jay said in a sleepy voice. The voice I had been thinking about all morning.

"Why have you been asleep for so long? You have no idea what just happened! My psycho sister set me up to meet my aunt at her office in Gurgaon. As depressing as a morgue that place," I continued to rant as I took a long drag from my cigarette.

"I could kill someone right now, Jay. Look at the hot weather. I hate summers! What a sad place! I hate corporate offices!" I went on my second rant with Jay within twelve hours. However, he seemed to be taking it well.

"Now, I think this rant is real, unlike the one you went on last night." He laughed. "Why would you even want to work as a corporate Alisha? It's sad!"

"Jay, I have to get a job till I have an execution plan. I want to have my own gig. I don't want to work for someone my whole life. Especially, if I have to dress up in one colour every day."

"Then what's stopping you?" He always asked good questions.

"I'm not ready yet. I guess I'm just waiting for the moment when I feel like a normal person."

"So, I was right. You *are* dealing with something?"

"Who isn't?" I asked.

"Fair enough. Well, I am not really a chatty person who would call people up. I couldn't resist today so I hope it's okay. Last night was good, I've never done this before." Wow, he was thinking about me too. I wasn't expecting that.

"I am glad you called, I kept thinking about you this morning," I said softly, with a huge smile on my face taking a puff from my cigarette.

He got weird after my reply. "Hmm, text you later?" he hung up. He flipped in a second. There was something off about this guy. Sometimes I wondered if he was a bot being operated by the *we-hate-sweet-gestures organization*.

I lied about having a great time at Tina Aunty's office to my family so they would stop bothering me for some time and spent the rest of the day watching documentaries on 9/11 and bingeing on chocolates. My life was practically at ground zero.

AN UBER AND A NERD

As the night hit, Jay called again. I was surprised. I had only blabbered to him until now. Was he into rants? Did he have a weird fetish?

"Should I be surprised that you're calling me?" I answered.

"Are you into scary movies at all?" The random question came from the other end. His goddamn voice!

"What? No way! I am the biggest coward I've met."

"Okay, so do you like hookah?" Jay asked hastily. His head was a mystery to me.

"Well, I am trying to quit smoking so…Why?"

"Weather is good nowadays, yeah? I really like the Italian they serve at this rooftop restaurant in Chanakyapuri," he said in a muffled tone, trying to keep it lowkey.

So many random thoughts. What did he want?

"Jay, What's wrong with you?"

"Alisha, I am trying to ask you out." I sat up straight as soon as he said that. A huge smile on my face. I was sure it was an involuntary movement.

"Woah, what?!" I cracked into subtle laughter. "I thought you were playing 20 questions with me again."

"And you successfully killed the whole vibe. Leave it. Dumbass." He was disappointed.

"Hey hey, smartie, don't blame me if you don't know how to ask a girl out."

"Yea, I don't have a lot of experience here, Ms Mehra."

Wait, how does he know my last name? My tinder profile only shows my first name. My brief pause of wonder made Jay quickly deflect from the topic.

"I have a conference in Poland next week. I'm excited about it."

"Wow. So are we just going to pretend that you haven't stalked me yet? Anyway, what will you get me from Poland?" I knew he would hang up as soon as I'd make him confess to stalking me so I turned.

"My friend Janelle, a local, makes homemade vodka. I'll fetch a bottle just for you!"

Even though I was not into vodka, I had to show excitement. Why god, why did he have to be a vodka person?

"Janelle?" I asked.

"Vodka is good for a celebration. And guess what? It reminds me that it's my birthday tomorrow," Jay said it like it was no big deal whatsoever.

"What? So, It's Mr-Change-The-Topic's birthday!"

"Well, I was trying to ask you out. I thought it would be a good idea to finally take a day off from work on my birthday."

"Shit. I didn't know Jay! Let's do this!" I sucked at math but I did all sorts of calculations in my head. "DLF Emporio at 11?" I asked excitedly.

"Can I pick you up?" Jay replied, saying each word with extreme care.

"So, is it like a date?"

"Alisha, don't make it harder for me than it already is. You know how I am. I don't know how to say all that."

"Okay okay! See you tomorrow then, loser!" I said playfully.

"Today. It's already midnight!"

"Happy birthday, Jay!" I could feel a thousand feelings rushing out as I wished him softly.

"I am glad it started with you. See you." It was a moment. Our first moment.

What was wrong with this guy? I would have been shouting out to the skies weeks before had it been my birthday. How was he so quiet about it? Every bit of sleep and frustration from Tina aunty's horror had left me. I was now sitting on my bed filled with excitement and planning.

I was meeting Jay. It was our first date and it was his birthday. He had never taken a day off from work and this was the first time he was celebrating his day. I was feeling a zillion butterflies in my stomach after such a long time. They had turned into dead moths over the last few months but I was feeling again. This was different.

Early next morning, I woke up to bake him a fresh batch of chocolate muffins. Cooking and baking gave me more pleasure than anything else. Surprisingly, I wanted to impress him. I pictured his reaction to my muffins throughout the morning. Would he eat them or would he take them home? Would he get happy or would he just put them aside?

"Hey mom, I am going for a job interview today! I'll be late! Like late evening." I walked up to mom as I wanted it to sound like a last-minute plan.

"Alright, but will it go on for the whole day?" My mom asked.

"Yeah, they have multiple rounds like GD and written tests and all." I was getting good at excuses, I thought to myself.

"And who are you baking for?"
Fuck. Think Alisha.
"Inaya! She will be there as well!" I have used her to cover my dates for years.
"Okay, have this curd and jaggery before you leave."
Jay will be here any minute and I already smelt like jaggery. Shit. I was running here and there trying to get everything perfect.
I texted Jay.

Where are you, birthday boy?

Sorry, my cab is stuck real bad in traffic. I'll be there in 30 mins.

Cab? Why are you coming to pick me up in a cab? I could've met you at the mall!

I was so confused.

Alisha, I don't know how to drive. I don't have a car. We never had a car.

I had four cars in my house and he was coming to pick me up in a cab. I was not accustomed to this kind of treatment. I could see so many questions spinning around my head like the rings on Saturn.
As I rinsed my mouth and checked myself in the mirror multiple times, he texted me.

I'm 5 mins away.

I made my way down the stairs. It was too sunny. He was wrong about the weather. And he did not come in 5 minutes. He took 20. I had roasted myself in the sun waiting for him. Triggering my anger, again.

15 minutes later, I saw an Uber Wagon-R approaching. It was cute. He did his best to be chivalrous. But he was late!

I smiled gently as I struggled to hold the batch of muffins, my big bag, shades, keys and mobile phone. This was how Jay saw me the first time. My clumsiest self. I had evolved into a classic who could hold all these things in one hand using a set of fingers due to the lack of pockets in any of my clothes. One thing each in a finger gap. Trust me, girls can do this.

Jay was cute! All nerdy, big glasses, hair pulled back, black clothes, wearing an Assassin's Creed t-shirt. The only thing that made him look hot was his beard. I wished he wouldn't hug. I was an awkward hugger. "You are late! I hate you," I complained as he approached to hug me.

"You are right! You are much fatter than I had expected." This was how Jay was. He would attack you before you could attack him for something he had done with such a wit that you just couldn't help but laugh. We started bantering.

"What! You cannot say that! WTF?" I flung my stuffed hands into the air. It was physically possible.

"Hahaha, come. Let's go, I have planned the whole day." He opened the door as I sat inside the cab.

HAPPY BIRTHDAY, JAY

I stared at Jay as he sat next to me looking outside the window. I wondered what was going on inside his head. He was so simple, yet beautiful. He was calm and wasn't trying hard. All the guys I'd ever dated would usually be dressed in their best, entertaining me with pathetic pickup lines by now.

I slowly pulled out the muffins from my bag. "Happy Birthday, Jay!" I smiled as I handed him the box. I waited eagerly for his reaction.

"What? I told you about my birthday at like midnight. Where did you find these?"

"Buddy, I baked them for you. You deserve a good birthday present."

"Wow, that's insane." He seemed awkwardly surprised almost questioning me why. His eyes did the rest of the talking and then he got impatient.

He opened the box hurriedly and stuffed his mouth with almost half of the big muffin. "Wow, Alisha. I love cupcakes. These are the best! Thanks, dude!"

"I'm glad you like them, though these are muffins, not cupcakes." Watching him eat so happily made me smile like I had seen a baby.

"There's a difference?" Jay was unbothered and surprised by this new revelation.

"I have not even tasted them, can I have some?" I asked, reaching for the box.

"No way! I'm going to save these and eat them for the next whole week! These are mine!" He said as he stuffed the box inside his bag, hiding it completely.

The radio played old Bollywood songs from the 80s. He sang them in pure pleasure and I played along. It was so easy to lose myself in those calm melodies.

"You know what, it's my first ever day off from work. It's the first time I am even celebrating the day," he confessed, gazing at me.

"Yeah, you told me but I don't believe you." Of course, I didn't.

"Trust me. You'll know," he said as he closed his eyes and laid back enjoying songs on the radio while we both sang together. I had not felt this relaxed in a very long time.

"You know, you look cute." He suddenly turned to me.

"I know right!" I didn't know how to respond to compliments. I have never been good at it. 'You're cuter!' I wanted to tell him but I choked on my words.

We reached the mall and it looked like a well-kept wilderness. We were the first visitors there. The store employees gave us judgemental glares. We were at Delhi's largest shopping mall at 11 am.

As we sipped our coffee at the cafe, Jay told me he had booked us movie tickets at the premium lounge. He had got me there in a cab and now we were spending money worth a lavish lunch on 2 movie tickets. Unbelievable.

"I know you must be thinking I'm trying to impress you with the whole gold class thing but honestly, I rarely do these things. And if I choose to do them I try to not compromise." He explained to me as if it needed an explanation.

"It's not my first time here. Which movie are we watching?"

"Well, it's my first time here. It's a fun movie. It is called IT."

These things about Jay fascinated me. But he could be lying, people lie.

"Isn't it scary?"

"Not at all."

As we sat through the movie, he was excited. I was nervous. I was not someone who could withstand ghosts or anything spooky. The movie started with a freaky clown in 3D.

"WTF Jay. I told you I cannot watch scary movies," I whispered to him.

"Trust me, you'll enjoy this one." His eyes shone in the dark. It was the way he looked at me, it was like his eyes were telling me a thousand stories. How did he do that?

As soon as the magic of his eyes turned away, I felt like a cat stuck inside a dark room. The creepy clown was now haunting little children. Unable to contain myself I let out a loud pitched scream.

He laughed a little and hesitantly reached for my hand trying not to look at me.

I swear to god, after months of abuse, molestation and slaughtered faith, I had forgotten how it felt like to be touched with care. I could see that his only intention then was to make me feel safe, which he did. His hand in mine felt like two waves intertwined. I never wanted to leave it.

We laughed through the rest of the movie.

Jay is not harmful. I told myself but a little part of me tried to resist this thought.

As the movie ended, the theatre lit up and he started to let go of my hand. I had this urge to not let it happen. As he got up, I grabbed his hand. He gave me a questionable look.

Quick, think of something Alisha.

"Umm, it's too dark. I don't want to fall in front of that cute guy at the back." I covered my act smartly pointing to a random guy in the row behind us.

Jay chuckled.

"What's the point if you're holding some other guy's hand in front of him?"

"Just because there's a goalie, doesn't mean he can't score." I outwitted him instantly.

"That was savage. Marry me, man." He laughed.

I felt a thud in my heart. I wanted to marry someone like Jay.

Stop Alisha. Stop imagining a wedding with every guy you meet. I kept reminding myself.

Jay took me to his favourite restaurant for lunch. He made me order. I ordered my best, a chocolate shake and chilli chicken. For him, I knew he liked pasta, so chicken alfredo it was.

Hand in hand, we discussed everything from his family to his work. Surprisingly, Jay opened up about his childhood.

"I've had a tough childhood. I went to those schools where you sit on the floor with slates and chalks. I used to walk to my university because we could not afford the bus fare." He smiled as he went down memory lane. "Never had those dreamy childhoods as you see in commercial movies, you know," Jay expressed his innermost thoughts. "Getting a bar of chocolate was occasional and burgers or ice creams were only allowed on festivals. I did not travel the world. I just found my interest, made it my passion and worked bloody hard for it."

I gazed at him listening intently. I was so moved.

As he brushed my hand softly, he continued. "Now I have a company of my own, running with 32 employees. I am still not making enough money but I sure as hell can offer you good dates." He knew I was getting serious, so he had to make it lighter.

"Wow. It must have been hard."

"Of course, multiple failures. It has not been easy to make a business of my own. My mom and dad are still doing multiple jobs to support us. One day, I want to build a good house for them, so they can rest. I want to do it for my future family, so my wife does not have to see what my sister and my mom have seen. I want to make it big. These dreams are what I live for," Jay said.

"Who doesn't? I have the same thinking. I want to be an entrepreneur too and so do many people around me. I would never have the guts to do it on my own. It is truly impressive how far you've come."

"How about you? How was your childhood?" He asked.

"Oh, I went to one of the most expensive schools, and universities. Had a very privileged life. Travelled abroad for studies. Now looking for jobs with people like you. So, can't compare myself to you in any way." I laughed softly.

"Come on, you have a Louis Vuitton bag on you right now, and a watch from a brand I can't even pronounce. Many people like you don't need to work or build careers. They usually take the easier route. You are working hard, I know. So, I don't think you are any different than me."

"No one looks at this like that." I was shocked to see how simply he had just uplifted my self-esteem. Those TEDx talks happened for a reason.

"This world brings you down. Don't look at them. Repulse. They will ask you what you do for a living just to calculate the amount of respect they gon' give you, be far away from that," Jay said sternly. "I took you out in a mediocre cab, I do not look like much, I don't belong to your group of friends probably. But here you are holding my hand and listening to me. This does not happen with me every day," he said as he stared deep into my soul.

The waiter interrupted us with the food. I took a deep sigh of relief because it was getting intense.

"Umm, what's vegetarian?" Jay asked the server.

"Oh…are you a vegetarian?"

"Umm…" He stared at the food for 20 seconds wondering what's what. "Nah, I can do chicken. It's fun."

"Fun?" I raised my brows in surprise.

"Come on, it's not like I haven't tried it before," Jay said while he served me some food.

I screwed up. He picked out all the chicken and bell pepper from the pasta, two of my favourite things.

After our very nice and fun meal, where he opened up to me about his family, we flirted with each other in good jest. While I returned from the loo, he had settled the bill.

"You didn't have to do that!" I exclaimed.

"I would have split but you see, I had been saving up for the right date. Had it not gone well, I would have made you pay."

Jay and his jokes.

"So, is this your thing? Talking to girls about your family and childhood and making them think that it's real?"

"No, usually I do throw in that I have two ex-girlfriends and both of them triple dated while they were with me. It adds value."

"Triple dated?! Ha-ha, loser!" I mocked him.

None of us wanted this date to end, so we moved on to a doughnut parlour. My favourite place.

"What's your story, Alisha?" Jay said as he devoured his vanilla creme doughnut.

"As I told you earlier, I had Abheer, who cheated on me with my friend. That's all."

"Come on, this can't be it."

"I like two sugars in my coffee, this is one. Could you please?"

Jay smirked at me as if he knew what was up.

After sharing countless stories and endless laughs, we called it a day.

He took my hand in the cab, "Alisha, the things I have told you today, I never usually talk about them. Let's make it a point that we never discuss them."

"You got it," I assured him, tightening my grip.

"I am surprised. After two failed relationships in college, I never really paid attention to any girl or opened myself up. I was so engrossed in my work that I didn't even go home often. I was so far away from this world of romance or any kind of relationship."

"Umm, okay, Jay. I get it. We all have our walls up."

"Alisha, all I am saying is that before you expect anything, I am not here for a relationship."

My heart somehow sank, I was not looking for a relationship either but was I just another date to him? Though why shouldn't I be?

"Bro, I get it. It's chill." I faked an affirmation

So much silence and inattentive scrolling on Instagram took place at both ends. Even the cab driver was staring at us after the dramatic confession. My cousin Advait, texted me. We had a rule. We knew about each other's dates and whereabouts at all times. The rule was a safety measure considering our reckless habits. I texted him back.

```
I think this is the guy who will teach me how
to love again.
```

"Cheating on me already? Who are you texting?" Jay noticed I was texting someone.
"My cousin."
"Of course. Yeah right!" Jay rolled his eyes at me.
"See, here." I showed him my chatbox.
Jay read my text. He looked deep into my eyes. It was a moment where we both knew what was coming. He leaned in. Damn.
My heart raced as he kissed me. After the five longest seconds of my life, I pulled back. My mind was empty and all the blood in my veins had gushed into my guts.
I pulled back because this always spoiled all my relationships. I was starting to fall for him, but low-key, I needed a friend more. I was confused while my walls had started caving around Jay.
As soon as I reached home, Jay left a text with a picture we had just taken.

```
It was the best birthday and the best date ever.
Thanks, Als.
```

```
Happy birthday again, Jay. Good night.
```

Even if Jay was trying to get close to me, I had decided to repulse. I knew how it would end. I knew how it would all end. I didn't sleep that night. I was constantly battling my feelings. I liked him a little more than I would have allowed myself to and now I had to find a way to get rid of it.

AUTO PILOT

Weeks passed and Jay and I were closer than ever. Our chemistry was unbeatable. I had started being happy, eating good food and hanging out with people. I was not worried about being hurt anymore. I was living in the moment. With Jay. He was sweet, simple and caring; a miracle in my life which had given me my reasons again. And so I let him in.

I got called for interviews at various companies. Somehow, talking to Jay was helping me bury my agony and live a normal life. I was myself, again. The hurt and the pain were so deep inside, I could not even sense them around.

I was hoping to rebuild myself with whatever remained of me.

I almost secured a job at Pestle Inc. - one of the most sought-after multinational corporations. I happily got dressed for my final interview. I left the house with my mom, who was chanting her prayers in the background but did not forget to feed me her famous curd and jaggery before I left.

I got into the car, feeling hopeful and confident, humming to my favourite Blues when my phone rang.

It was Alec, my confidante from the USA who never forgot to wish me on my important days.

"Hey, bunny!" I might have sounded happier than usual.

"How's my bunny doing now?"

"How do I sound? I am so happy, man. Jay and I spoke all night long. He is so funny. It is after so long that I have felt connected with someone. It can't get any better."

"Alisha, what's wrong with you? Don't you have an interview in like 45 minutes?" Alec sounded worried.

"Yeah, I'm on my way."

"And you're thinking about Jay? How can you be more excited about a boy than your interview at Pestle?"

"He is not any random boy, Alec. He makes me happy. We have to give him some credit, right?"

"Get out of your little bubble, Ally. He is just another boy who held your hand and made you laugh. He has done nothing. You just gave him extra credit because you were lonely. Look at things objectively."

"Alec, I am not ready for this right now. You know I really like him."

"Yeah, you need to realize you only like him because he is not like Abrar or Abheer. You need to set yourself straight, Alisha. You cannot fall for this guy. He has set his priorities about not wanting a relationship straight." Alec tried his best to safeguard me.

"We all know his thing against relationships is temporary. Don't spoil my mood now. I got to go." That was the best I could do.

"Fine. Do well at the interview and call me afterwards."

"Okay. Thanks," I hung up, disappointed.

But I knew Alec was right. I was only feeling affectionate towards Jay because I was vulnerable and desperate. I shouldn't be taking things so seriously.

My phone rang again. Jay. Worst timing ever.

"Yeah?" I answered in a dull voice.

"What's wrong? Hope you've reached?"

"Yeah, I will, in 10 minutes."

"Alisha, are you nervous? Why are you so low?"

"Yeah, just nervous I guess."

"You're my rockstar. Come on! A big smile and lots of confidence. Forget everything else."

"Hmm, okay," I hung up.

Alec's words occupied a large part of my mind that day. Will Jay never agree to be with me? Was this another heartbreak waiting to happen?

As I reached Pestle's office, I parked my car and started making my way towards the front desk. On my way, sitting on a bench was Jay.

"Jay, what are you doing here?" I exclaimed. I could feel the whole damn zoo in my belly.

"Hey, cupcake. Here's some coffee. Two sugars. Thought you could use some."

"We just talked! How did you even?"

"My office is nearby so yesterday when you told me about this interview, I planned to pop up."

"Jay, please stop being so sweet." I felt embarrassed.

Jay looked at my face questionably because he was expecting me to be surprised, not disappointed.

"I have to run now," I said, avoiding his eyes. "I'll text you later."

"Als, wait!" Jay stopped me with a worried frown on his face. I stopped and turned to him. "What?"

"Nail it!" Jay said as he hugged me tightly.

Again, I lived a hundred years in that hug. I loved his hugs. I left without responding.

Crediting my luck which made me jump from one problem to another, I ran into a classmate from university at the interview candidates line-up.

"Hey," we greeted each other in a fake manner.

"So, good to see you, Alisha! Your skin has cleared up."

"Excuse me?"

"I am surprised to see you here. I thought you had decided to make a living by telling people fake stories about how a sweet guy like Abrar molested you."

"That's none of your business," I told her, acting like none of her words affected me.

"A few months ago, it was everybody's business at the campus."

I wish I could give her a fitting reply but felt too weak. *Just focus on the interview, Als. Focus.*

I was the first one to be called in for the interview. I thanked my stars.

The interviewers were very impressed with me. They liked my crisp and straightforward answers. As Jay had said, "I nailed it."

As soon as I came out, she asked me how it went.

"It's tough. They are expecting twisted answers. The more you speak the better."

For some reason, interviews had never been a difficult feat for me. I had always been vocal about things that mattered to me, and that worked well for interview rounds. As I called my mom on my way out and unlocked my car, Jay stood there. With my favourite Theobroma Macaroons in his hands.

I looked at him in disbelief.

"If it went well, these are to celebrate, if not, they'll help you feel better so..." He said, hesitatingly.

"Jay! You idiot!" I hugged him as tight as I could. "I can't believe you are still here, waiting for me!"

"Weirdly enough, I can't believe it too."

After we spent an hour by the fountain park, hand in hand, we laughed till our bellies hurt. As he held my hand, I felt like all the nerves in mine, reached straight to my heart. I had never felt anything more.

He took me to his office and introduced me to his friends and colleagues. It was a very happy day after such a long time. How could I resist this? It was like a rainbow and all the colours led to him.

I had not even reached home when Pestle called me. I had been accepted. My family celebrated that evening. My mom thanked her curd and jaggery, as we all laughed.

Tina aunty also called me that night. Not to congratulate me but to tell me that she had another offer for me in Gurgaon. I googled the company, it was right next to Jay's office!

He texted me around 2 am.

```
Als! My friends can't stop talking about you. You
look good in formals.
```

```
Ha-ha, thanks. Which one particularly? I liked
the bearded fellow in HR.
```

```
Did you hear from Pestle?
```

He changed the topic to hide his jealousy, I hoped.

```
Yeah, I didn't get it.
```

I lied.

That sucks! Why though? It's their loss!

I got a better opportunity instead. It's right next to your office.

I wanted more time with him. After every heartbreak, I'd tell myself that I was just another heartbreak closer to my happily-ever-after. And now, Jay felt like my happily-ever-after. I accepted Tina Aunty's offer. For the first time ever, I was grateful to her.

Months passed. I was doing well. I was winning clients, getting awards and I was a kickass employee. Soon, people started recognizing me in the industry. I loved my work and I was excelling at it too.

Jay started travelling to countries for his talks and writing books. We were both so proud of each other. We kept one another going. Life was good. As John Green once said, *I fell in love like you would fall asleep: slowly and then all at once.*

By the evening he would come and we would talk for hours at the terrace of my office building. Endless coffee dates, lunches, night-ins. He would get me a bottle of local vodka from every country he would visit and then we would book hotel rooms to celebrate our success.

All of them ended with us getting happily drunk and passing out together while cuddling in the bathtub. We never crossed our limits though. We never needed to. We enjoyed our platonic relationship enough. My heart was full.

I was smitten and mothered by his simple yet charming self who would never lose control or give in to his desires. He respected me, my insecurities and my limitations. Until now, I had only fantasized about such a thing.

As months passed happily with Jay, I was consistently ignoring my deteriorating health. I knew something was wrong with me but I was happy after a very long time. I wanted to keep it that way and not let anything worry me.

I could list my symptoms which were getting worse by the day. Missed cycles, a painful abdomen, cystic acne, unexplained weight gain, lactose resistance, hormonal imbalances, screwed up insulin levels. My muscles were so weak, I could barely brush my teeth without my arm giving up. I wish I'd paid attention to them earlier.

I finally realised the severity of the situation when I went to work after a morning workout session with normal exercise pain, but a few hours later, I could not even walk. I came home in a wheelchair.

My doctors thought it was a common case of PCOS and put me on hormonal medication. As I had said, my life had never been simple.

One night, I woke up screaming in agony. I was in so much pain. My lower abdomen was killing me. I could feel it in my guts. I was sweating all over. The pain had increased so much, I could barely stand straight. I texted Jay.

Something's wrong.

Jay was in Amsterdam; we were in different time zones.

I returned from the States thinking I had left the worst behind. I had buckled up, wanting to move forward. And even though I continued to grieve every once in a while, I thought I was being offered a flicker of hope within Jay. I was starting to believe that maybe there was a way to fight all of it and to carve my own destiny. But here I was, crumbling again as a result of my past. My screams of pain were so loud, my parents ran to my room. Mom knew I had to be rushed to the hospital. It was the scariest night of my life. I thought I would die.

After seven days of tests, imaging, and unbearable pain, I was diagnosed with Cervical Cancer.

Do you know that feeling when you just lose all your senses for a moment? A sharp beep in your head is all you're capable of discerning? It was like that until I was back home. Numb. I bet the world kept moving around me, but all I could see were still images. As if I was dead already, existing within a non-living thing. All blank and frozen.

My parents quietly put me to bed but sat outside my room for hours. I could hear my mom crying. How could I put them through something like this? My body was giving up on me. I had fought many battles, but could I fight this one? I had never felt more shook or scared.

Days passed but I was still numb inside. I was talking, eating, laughing on the outside, but I was not in a position to discuss this with anyone or realise it myself. My last text to Jay had been *Something's wrong* and he had made endless efforts to reach me. I was just too disappointed in life to open up to anyone at all. I couldn't gather enough courage to tell him.

When I wanted to die, life didn't let me and now that I was starting to live, life won't let me.

Alec had also realised that I was not in a good state. I wasn't responding to him or anyone else. His semester had just ended. After 3 months of this revelation, Alec was there at my doorstep one morning.

WHAT SISTERS DO

Our doorbell rang, and I walked towards the door cam while rubbing my eyes out of sleep.

"Is that..? What...? What the hell?" I exclaimed as I couldn't believe my eyes. This was the first time my parents were seeing me cry since the diagnosis.

I sprinted towards him. He was looking around wondering if he was at the right address.

Dressed in his comfy sweatshirt, there stood Alec after a whole year. I couldn't help but notice my black necklace around his wrist.

"Alec? What are you doing here!?" I flung my arms around him. Suddenly, we were back to our last night at Lytle's creek.

"Alisha, who is it?" My father was so confused.

Alec and I were hugging out a thousand untold stories that very moment while my parents simply stared.

"Dad, this is my best friend, Alec. We studied together in California."

Alec, being the sweetheart that he was, got gifts for everyone.

"So, what do you do, Alex?" My father said in a very serious tone while we all sat in the guest lounge. My parents were very sceptical of us and like every conservative Indian family, doubted us to be a couple. But we were like siblings, which was hard for them to fathom.

"I just graduated, Uncle. I am applying for a bank job in London after this. Also, uncle, it's Alec," he said with a lot of patience.

"Dad, he is like a brother to me. I am so happy he is here. Alec, you made my day!" I was the happiest I could ever be. He was my silver lining.

My mom brought in snacks and tea for Alec and then swiftly took my dad away to the side for a minute. Alec and I continued chatting about the university and our friends. Akira, for some reason, did not join us and stayed in the corner.

For my parents, strict rules were very well defined. They had never let any of my male friends come home or sit with me in my room before. However this time, my mom surprisingly asked him to stay with us. I was ecstatic but I also knew that my mom only did this because I was sick. Terribly sick.

In the evening, Alec and I were hanging out at our home theatre when dad called me.

"Alisha, why don't you let Akira join you guys. She didn't like it when you said Alex was the sibling you never had. Come here, talk to her and tell her you didn't mean to hurt her." I put two and two together and figured my sister was feeling jealous.

"We all know exactly what I meant, Dad. Fine! I am coming up in two minutes." I left the theatre disappointed.

I walked up to Akira, who was sitting with our parents and sobbing like a victim.

"Hey, I am sorry you felt bad. Come join us." I shook my head as I tried to console her with my empty and meaningless apology.

"You better be. Alex will never be what I am."

I felt confused about why Akira was suddenly feeling so left out. She had always been distant to me and these comments suddenly made me feel angry at her. I had never expected support from my sister, but these were extraordinary circumstances.

"Listen. His name is Alec, not Alex."

"Alisha, come on. We have respected him enough. I have never brought a guy home, and see, mom and dad, allow you to do everything! You get everything while I never do." Akira went on.

"You're not the one who's dying. Stop pitying yourself for a second!" I screamed at her for the first time.

"Alisha! Shut up!" My mom appeared from the background and asked me to leave.

"No mom. You listen to me. Akira was never a sister. She was never there for me. She has never done anything for me whereas I have given her everything you have ever expected me to."

After a long pause of really uncomfortable silence in the room, I continued expressing what needed to be said.

"Where was she when I had issues at school? Where were you all? Did you know I had problems at work? Every time I try getting closer to you, you throw me away. Even after I got diagnosed, my darling sister never spoke to me about it. How is she a sister, papa? A month ago, I was suicidal. You do not know that, because you do not care enough! You cannot beg for my attention and respect; you need to earn it. I am done giving my all and getting nothing in return. I have issues too. I need to be heard too."

"Akira, I skipped a whole freaking semester because you needed me here for your wedding which you very conveniently postponed because of a stupid venue. Would you do that for me? Every time I try to talk to one of you, you avoid it because our darling Akira here feels left out. Akira, we are siblings! Learn to share. They are my parents too. You can not compete with me for their attention. You are insecure and you find satisfaction in manipulating them. You need to fix your issues and stop creating new ones for me, please!" The words flushed right out my mouth.

My parents were furious, and an eerie silence followed.

"Enough! Enough of your nonsense! That boy out there has poisoned your mind!" My father couldn't hold back his rage. He was trying to control the situation by shutting me up.

"He hasn't dad. All he has done is fix me. He has picked up all my pieces one by one while you all chose to ignore them. He has held my secrets, sister! He has filled the void you have created inside me. He has done everything you should have done, big sister. You have done nothing but put me down by manipulating others. Alec cares enough to travel overseas for me, you don't even cross a hallway for me Akira. He is the sibling I never had and I mean it!"

I stormed out of the room and this time I was not going to cry. She needed to get out of her delusional thoughts. She needed to realize what she had done. Alec was waiting for me. Someone, who had flown halfway across the world to hear me out.

REVELATION AND REALIZATION

It was my favourite time of the day again, nightfall. Alec and I sat by the garden and stirred our favourite cocktails, which he made. He listened to me while I was going on and on about Akira.

"Als, I know this is the worst time to bring it up, but it's important that I tell you something," Alec said while he tried to look at me.

I looked at him wondering what he was about to say.

"I don't know where Abrar is."

I suddenly looked away because even his name scared me.

"Alisha, you're safe. It's him who needs saving. Don't worry."

"Why are you telling me this? Why would I care?" Alec's sudden mention of Abrar had resurrected the monster inside me. I felt a strong temptation to smash the glass in my hand.

"The last time I saw him he wanted to make sure if you were okay."

"What? What the fuck, Alec?" I was disappointed in Alec. "I don't want to know," I fumbled.

I felt like a thousand bees had stung me in my back. I didn't want to be here. I suddenly wanted to be alone. I was panicking. I pulled out a cigarette from Alec's pack and lit it up. Even the simple mention of his name was enough to give me chills.

"I had to tell him about us, Ally. He was mad at first but since he didn't see you before you left, he just wanted to make sure you were…"

"Dead?" I interrupted him sternly.

"Healthy."

Nobody spoke for the next 5 minutes. I had finished the whole cigarette and reached out for another. I knew it could kill me.

"Alec. I am not healthy. You can go and tell this to your 'friend' and rejoice."

Alec came closer, he pulled up my sleeve to check on some wounds I had, courtesy of Abrar.

"They are mere scars now, Alec. They'll go. Don't worry." I slid down my sleeve, battling to hide them. "I need to sleep. If you need anything, please let the maid know." I walked away with tears brimming in my eyes.

I knew going to sleep was a lie. Even though my remains had made it past the long haul, numbing me in the process, there were times when they bit back; especially during the night. I may have healed enough from my past to turn the pictures into black and white, but the fact remained that they existed. Inside my head. Like the undead just waiting to feed on my soul through even the smallest gaps I would leave ajar.

"Als, Inaya's with him."

Again, the high pitched beep in my head. I couldn't think of anything.

"You said you would take care of her. Is she.." I asked with a straight face.

"I don't know, I am sorry but she decided to leave with him." Alec's face brimmed with nervousness.

"In that case, I don't care. You came all the way to tell me that?" I stormed out of the garden without waiting for an answer. I felt betrayed. Defeated.

I was walking to my room when I ran into the corner of the hallway and broke down. Inaya and Abrar had a history which was enough to break me down.

I could hear someone approaching. I wiped my tears as fast as I could. "Oh, so toy boy made you cry? Like you made me tonight? My wedding got postponed because of your cancer thingy. Don't you ever say I never made any sacrifices for you," Akira said.

At that moment, I could finally feel my whole world come crashing down. I was dying. I felt unwanted by my family. My best friend had just stabbed me in the back and the only guy I had started to trust, was not sure about what he needed. That was it. I had hit rock bottom. Again.

I spent the whole night sulking in a corner of my bathroom, smoking the whole pack of Alec's cigarettes. I kept thinking in circles. Why was I doing this? Why was I even alive? I had no reason to be here. I was too weak for this now.

The scars on my arms, my torso and the places I had been hiding from the world, filled me with agony. They were nothing but a killing reminder of my shame, my grief. I hated my skin. I hated his scars on my skin. I picked up the sharpest blade out of vanity and scraped them one by one. The stream of blood from each scar felt like novocaine fixing the pain inside my heart. I wanted to see how much it bled, how much I still had it in me. However, it only went as far as this. I had tried to finish the parts of me that still lingered on, looking for freedom. I spent the whole night in regret, agony and self-loathing. Around 6 am, my dad came into my room to check up on me. He had been doing that ever since my diagnosis. I was half-conscious in a pool of blood and sweating profusely.

I spent the next month in the hospital trying to heal my chest as much as my body. My family spent a whole lot of money on treating my medical issues but nobody cared about my unhealthy mind. I didn't want to get up from that hospital bed. I wanted it to open its jaws and swallow me in.

Alec had returned to America and I was quitting every day.

After more than three weeks, I had a visitor. It was Jay.

He could not see me like this. With whatever strength I had, I got up and pulled my hair into a ponytail. Without any makeup, I managed to pull out a lip balm from my sanitary bag. Lots of hand crème. People hold sick people's hands. Jay always holds my hand. Gotta moisturize the shit out of these little bitches. Even my dead ass enthusiasm got hyped up around Jay.

"Maa, send him in…" I called for Jay as he had been waiting outside while I groomed myself.

"Alisha. Woah, you look ugly," Jay said as his eyes gleamed.

"Ugly without you. Come here you." I was so happy to see him.

He gently kissed my forehead. I flipped from being distant and disappointed to needy and hopeful.

"Are you dying?"

"Not yet. I choose to stay."

"This is hilarious. I heard you've turned into a person who has lost the will to live. You look quite fragrant to me."

I stayed silent. Did he know what had happened? How? How did he know I was here?

"Als, I am so hot for you right now. You've lost weight and these scrubs look sexy on you."

"Shut up! Who told you I was here?"

"I have my sources," he said as he pulled out a necklace from his pocket. This was my Westminster Abbey black necklace.

"I am not Abrar, Alisha. I am here to stay, as your best friend. You're getting up, fighting this and making a kickass boss lady out of yourself. Do you hear me?"

As soon as he said Abrar, I reckoned Alec had told him everything.

"You met Alec? Tell me what he told you."

Jay stared at my face, deep in thoughts.

"When you were moved to the ER that morning, leaving Alec in utter confusion, he enquired your sister about you. She told him everything. He got hold of me somehow and told me just enough, Als. You should speak to him," he looked at me with genuine kindness, but I was still mad at Alec.

"What did he tell you? How do you know Abrar?" I asked Jay in an angry tone.

"Why didn't you tell me about this earlier? I'd thought we could talk about anything." Jay was still trying to be empathetic.

"Jay stop it! I don't want to talk about this. I am good and I'll be home soon."

"How soon?"

"They terminated my contract at the company. I am jobless. Give me one reason why I should think of getting out of here."

"Because if you don't then I will have to find another media partner for my own company," Jay hinted at an offer.

"What?"

"You're the best publicist I know, Alisha. Come work with me. I already know your ethics and style. I'd kill to hire a publicist like you."

Was it a sign? Where was all this leading? I immediately started imagining what it'd be like to work with Jay. Be around him every day. It was magical.

"Jay, will it be healthy for us? Working together?" I asked.

"Come on, what could go wrong?" Jay shrugged slightly.

"I could fall in love with you."

"And how is that wrong?"

I felt a cluster of emotions inside me, almost like a tornado. It was weirdly calming.

He kissed my forehead gently.

"Can I ask you something, Alisha?"

This was it. He was going to do it.

"I like questions, remember?" I smiled as I vividly recaptured our first conversation.

He looked deep into my eyes. It was a numbing moment. I felt foolish, foolishly falling for him every moment.

"Any hot nurses around?" He slowly whispered in my ear.

"Asshole," I said as we broke into playful laughter.

A few days later as I was returning home, I went back in time to when I was returning from California. I had the same feeling this time; of burying all the horrors inside me and heading home with high hopes.

WHAT I CALL HOME

As I spent my day sitting in the garden, watching my rabbits rejoice, I sipped on Mom's jaggery tea. What was with my mom and jaggery? It made me smile, and I wondered why she and I had never really had a heart to heart talk. I had always craved for her attention. I wanted to know her better.

Maybe, it was because her firstborn wouldn't like it. I wished my sister would just tell me the wrongs I did to her, for once. So that I could fix them and have an actual life with my family. Akira was so particular about her place in the family, I never once had a hearty chat with anyone. I was bullied through school, heartbroken, abused, beaten up, insulted and made fun off, and now I was battling cancer without having anyone to talk to. What did I do so wrong Akira? It ached my heart every time I saw her just sulking away. I hated this rivalry. I just wanted a sister.

"Mom, can we talk?" I asked mom gently as I spotted her near the garden.

"Why are you here, Alisha? You'll exert yourself," she said as she caressed my hand.

"Why don't we ever talk, maa?" I looked straight into her eyes, looking for an answer.

"We do, what's wrong?"

"No, maa. I feel terribly alone. I can't fight this alone."

"We are all here for you," Maa started looking around, I knew her eyes searched for Akira.

"Is that it? Are you looking out for Akira?"

"My darling, look, Akira has always been insecure, she is not very strong-headed. When you were born, she felt very competitive. I still recall, dad used to come from work and take you in his arms before Akira. She hated it and became a resentful child. She started falling sick when the doctors advised us to look after her with extreme care."

"Mom, Akira was a kid then but she is 26, now!"

"Alisha, we need to take care of her and as we have seen, you are more independent. You usually handle things better alone. You are a stronger and much more self-sufficient individual."

I nodded as she hastily got up and escorted me to my bed.

"I don't know how this is justified. Can we please go out for lunch, once?"

"Do let me know if you need anything, I am cooking your favourite tonight." Mom smiled wide as she shut the door.

My mind was tired of trying to understand the logic behind her words. Was all this reasonable enough? I was a newborn, of course, dad wanted to hold me. I was dying, of course, they wanted to hold me again. With the heaviest rock on my heart, I took out my iPod and tuned in to Joe Rogan.

I picked up my phone and posted my first Facebook status.

I didn't choose to do it alone, I am just used to doing it alone.

Maybe Akira would see it and we would talk. Maybe, mom would see it. Maybe, just for once, someone would see it.

I had to make peace with it. It's good the way it is.

How's home? Miss you already.

A text from Jay.

I miss you too, Jay. Come over.

Excuse me? Are you asking me to meet your parents?

Actually, yes. You could talk to them about me working with you. There are some health restrictions and I think if you meet them, they'll trust you better.

What was I thinking? Bringing boys to this house was frowned upon.

Job proposal at a family dinner? Do you do anything the normal way?

I'll bake pasta with no pepper, just the way you like it.

Alisha, I can't. It's scary.

Why was he scared? I called him.
"We won't eat you!" I stressed as soon as he answered.

"I have met my friend's family earlier. This is different. Nope, I can't," Jay said in a low tone. His voice still sounded like music to my ears.

"Well, if you're so uncomfortable then okay. I can't force you. I will speak to them about the job."

"I do miss you, a lot. I can't stop thinking about the cuddles and all the passing out. We need to go away again."

"I think so too, but not anytime soon. I can't go out much until after a few weeks."

"Weeks?!" Jay sounded shocked.

"Yeah, why are you surprised?"

"Which shirt should I wear? Are y'all free tomorrow?"

My insides raced. I felt every bit of my blood gush to my legs. I was weak in my knees. "Jay, you know that I've never made them meet any of my guy friends right?"

"I will have to meet them one day or the other. Plus they know me from the hospital. They should know the guy their daughter is crazy about." I could hear the nervousness in his confident words.

"Okay, dinner tomorrow, at 8 PM?"

"Fuck, Als. This is big, but I need to see you somehow so whatever."

Every brick in my wall I had carefully laid in the past year came tumbling down. Jay was in.

Next morning, I woke up with the widest grin on my face, again. Jay was coming over. I was nervous. Would my parents be okay with this? I walked up to my mother, setting my game plan into motion. *Talk her up like you enter a cold shower. You'll be hesitant initially but gradually it'll settle.*

"Morning, maa," I hugged her from behind. "Should I help you with breakfast today?"

"What? Are you sick again?" She touched my forehand with the back of her hand pretending to check my temperature.

"Very funny, Maa," I said sarcastically. "You do so much, I want to lend a hand." I started slicing up ginger for dad's tea.

"Aalu, what do you want this time? I can count your teeth with that huge smile on your face."

I chuckled as I pulled her aside. "Maa, remember the guy who visited me at the hospital? Jay Arora?"

"I like him," she smiled.

I was startled. I didn't even have to persuade her. "Excuse me?"

"Come on. The only time you put lip gloss in that stupid hospital was when he came to visit you. We were your age too, we know how this works." She pulled my cheek as I blushed.

"So, can he come over tonight? For dinner? At 8?" My voice was just a little too higher to be audible enough.

"You have already invited him, haven't you? I know you, my little impulsive meteorite."

"Mom, talk to dad no? I really want him to meet all of you." I chuckled.

"Consider it done."

I hugged her in utter excitement.

"You must not expect much from Akira, though," she said in a nervous tone.

"I get it maa. I don't want her to spoil this for me. I don't want anything from her. Just you and papa."

"I wish I could have supported you through everything, but I am going to make up for my shortcomings beta. I was wrong." She hugged me as tight as she could.

I wanted to tell her how much I loved her but sometimes telling that to someone is enough to ruin everything. I spent the whole day baking my best pasta and tiramisu. We, the conservative Mehra's, were having a boy over. This was all very new for us. My dad kept smiling at me the whole time. He realised I was growing up and was happy that mom and I had mended our ways.

"He likes vodka, you said?" Dad came out with his fanciest bottle of black vodka.

"OMG! He will love this!" I hurriedly placed the bottle carefully at the well-decorated dining table. My phone flashed with a text from Jay.

Als, I'm shitting my pants. This is nerve-racking. Been downstairs for 10 mins, can you come and get me?

Cutie.

Jay looked extraordinarily overdressed for a casual dinner. He wore a freaking jacket in August for heaven's sake.

"What's with the Harvey Specter look?"

"Do not make me more nervous than I already am, stupid." He handed me flowers, a box of chocolates and his phone, while he fixed his clothes and double-checked his shoelaces.

"Als, do you think I should have brought a bottle of wine?"

"Jay, why are you freaking out?"

"I really want them to like me. Look at your freaking house. Why do you have so many cars?"

I wanted him to shut up. Jay always compared our money to his. He was so insecure when it came to that.

As we reached upstairs, Jay's nervousness made him clumsy. He forgot to greet my mom and hugged my dad awkwardly long for some reason. I was laughing hard inside.

My parents had magically turned into the coolest parents ever. I thought to myself again. Was I dying?

"So, is he friends with Alec? I hope you do know Alec, Jay? Her friend who visits her across oceans which is unusual for normal friends to do," Akira said, walking out of nowhere.

My heart sank. Why was she trying to destroy this?

"Yes, in fact, we get along together well. Alec sends his regards." Jay was not nervous anymore, even though he had just lied.

"Akira, could you make yourself a little scarce, please. We had talked about this." I heard my dad whisper to her. What was happening? Had my Facebook status worked?

For the next hour, as my dad interrogated him, I just concentrated on Jay. Like a child, he gulped his pasta, washing it down with dad's finest vodka. I could see the nervousness on his face.

"So, you like to drink, huh?" Dad asked.

Jay froze. He almost seemed as if he didn't know what to say.

"Mr Mehra, to be honest. I am nervous as hell. I literally can't even swallow my food right now since my guts are in my throat. But it's yummy, aunty," he carefully covered up.

"I am here to ask you if I can take your daughter away to Mumbai for a couple of months so she can work with me. I really can't take a no on this, so my nerves are just getting the best of me. And yes, I drink when I am nervous."

Everybody stopped and stared at him. What did he just do? Regret and embarrassment lingered on Jay's face. He gave me a side-eye. I was shocked.

My parents looked at me and broke into loud laughter, and this was how Jay and I went away to Mumbai together.

DÉJÀ VU

One month later, I sat at Marvé Beach - one of the quietest beaches in Mumbai - with my cigarette flickering in the gentle breeze. Sand covered my bare feet, finding snug spaces between my toes. Dusk enveloped the remains of the day, preparing for the oncoming night. It was déjà vu from 2 years ago.

It was weird how I found myself back here, at this moment, thousands of miles and many months later. The world was ending once more. Once more, a dark storm was annihilating me. Twisted flames were consuming my existence and everything I was, everything I ever would be. Only, this time, there was no one else to blame. The betrayal had come by my own hand. My body was failing me, and I did not know what to do.

Maybe that was why I sought out the sea. The sound of the waves, lazily crashing upon the shore in strange music, was a far cry from the tempest that raged inside. I missed Alec, then, and the soothing companionship he brought with him.

"I thought I'd find you here." Jay's voice drifted from behind my shoulder. "You know that cancer stick isn't good for you."

I laughed as I pulled a drag, immersing myself into the hit. "You say the dumbest things. What's it going to do, kill me deader?"

"Kill you sooner," he replied, sitting down beside me. Dressed in a formal suit, blazer unbuttoned, Jay looked like a million bucks. But, when his eyes met mine, the sincerity in them caught me off-guard.

"I don't want to lose you, Als."

I rested my head on his shoulder. He smelled fresh, like musk, even after a long day. "I'm here, for now," I whispered, breathing in his heady scent. "That should be enough."

"It is." He kissed the top of my head. "For now."

We sat there for a while, the comfortable silence accompanied by ambient sounds as the world exhaled. I closed my eyes, breathing in the rhythm of everything around me: the changing timbre of the city, the wind's gentle caress upon my skin, the murmur of conversation from other beachgoers. The sea called out to me with its chaotic song, so strange, yet so familiar. The apocalypse in my soul subsided, if only for a moment.

It took me a while to realise that Jay was humming.

"What's that?" I asked.

"What? Oh," he said, realising with a start what he'd been doing. "Just a song I heard this morning that's been stuck in my head. Something about a room without light with crumbling walls."

I stiffened, trying not to react. The lyrics brought back memories of a time when I was in a dark room, scared, without any light or means to get out. No walls crumbled back then, just my sense of self.

He still noticed. "Did I say something wrong?" He turned to me, concerned written large upon his face.

"No, you didn't. It is fine," I said in as normal a tone as I could muster. "It's absolutely fine."

To someone as observant as Jay, that was a dead giveaway. "You alright, Als? I'm sorry if I said something upsetting. I didn't mean to do it."

I wanted to tell him that it wasn't his fault. How *could* he have known? I never shared the depth of the despair I carried, never discussed how constant it was, how crushing. I'd never opened up about Abrar or the abuse he had inflicted, or the wounds I'd received from the hands of those I loved long before that. He did not know that the only reason I still functioned was that I refused, every moment of every day, to give in. My scars run deep. My issues had become a part of who I was. And now I was dying.

I shook my head, unwilling to trust myself to speak, but a lone tear still escaped and traced its path on my cheek. Jay held himself from probing any further, even though his eyes were aflame with a thousand questions. Instead, he gingerly put his arm around me – caring yet cautious, familiar yet unwilling to assume it.

"Hey, Als. Whatever it is, it'll be okay," he said as he stroked my head. "We'll make it okay."

Without thinking, I gave into Jay's embrace. Deep, heaving sobs escaped from my body. His simple empathy had triggered something in me. The walls I'd erected so carefully, brick by brick, over the last several months, were tumbling. Emotions I thought I'd locked away forever – pain, anger, guilt, shame, agony – had flooded back with a vengeance. All the old scars in my soul flared with renewed intensity. Time heals all wounds, right? Bullshit.

By all reason, it should have overwhelmed me. I'd seen too much shit, had my trust broken too many times to even consider the possibility of a better future. Fate had played its cruel tricks before, lulling me in taking it all away. Why would this time be any different?

I don't know how long it lasted. I just remember that, through all of it, Jay held me tight. I didn't believe him when he said it would be all right. I didn't *want* to believe him. But, with each tear I shed, my burden lightened. I wasn't as numb to the pain as I'd have liked to be, but it didn't seem to hurt as much. There, sitting on the beach in his embrace, listening to the calming sound of the sea, I felt like I could truly find a way to heal.

When I finally looked up, I caught Jay's eye and chuckled, wiping away my tears. "You're such an idiot. It'll be okay, yeah? You don't even know what you're talking about!"

He laughed, playfully pushing me away. "That's rich coming from someone who's dribbled a bucketful of snot all over my suit. You're paying for the dry-cleaning." He looked at me once more with complete earnestness. "You sure you're okay, Als?"

I nodded. "Yes, I'm okay. I'm fine." I meant it. "Let's go back to the hotel. We need to talk."

IT STARTED WITH A BREAK-UP

"You do realise that 'we need to talk' is not something a normal person says to another person without major implications regarding the future?" Jay twirled the glass of whiskey in his hands with exaggerated care, as if caressing a lover.

We were in my hotel room. At my suggestion, we stopped at a Wine & Beer shop on our way back to pick up some alcohol. I needed liquid courage. We hadn't spoken much since my emotional breakdown at the beach. The small talk didn't count; it was a filler preceding a much weightier conversation which I didn't know how to begin.

I kicked the chair he was sitting on to express my irritation with his smart-ass comments. "You do realise that no part of either of us is what other people would call normal?"

He tilted his head in deliberation. "Hmm, fair enough," he said after a while. "So what was this thing you wanted to talk about? Don't tell me you're finally in love with me. As much as I'd love for that to be the case, I genuinely don't have the bandwidth for any entanglement right now."

That earned his chair another kick. "You wish that you were that lucky," I replied.

"I do, I do. You know I do."

The earnestness in Jay's voice had me off-balance for a moment. I never knew where I stood when he made these abrupt switches between flippancy and sincerity, never sure of what he was thinking or feeling. My objections didn't find any purchase; he brushed them off with a joke and said 'issues' as if that explained everything.

Well, screw his issues. We were here to talk about mine.

I took a sip of my drink. "Are you done?"

He grinned. "Not in the way I'd like to be. But, yes, please do continue. Where do you want to begin?"

It was a good question, and one I hadn't considered before. The episode with Abrar had cast a shadow across my entire life, colouring my perception of everything that had happened to me before or since. When *did* it all begin? When we first met in California? Or were the seeds of mistrust and hurt sown much earlier, during my ill-fated relationship with Abheer? I didn't know the answers. I didn't even know where to begin looking for them.

So I decided to put the ball in Jay's court. "What did Alec tell you?"

"Not much. He told me that you were carrying a lot of trauma from a previous relationship which was the reason behind your trust issues. He also mentioned that this guy, Abrar, was abusive." He looked at me, then, with intent. "It didn't seem polite to ask *how*."

To my surprise, my voice caught in my throat when I tried to reply. Did he pity me? Or was there curiosity behind that expression? A new scoop? Smooth as he was, Jay wasn't always as above such pettiness as he liked to project. Was his friendship an act to get me to trust him before he could break me in new ways?

"Does *how* really matter?" I asked, the tone flat and dry.

Jay's eyes had been fixed on me the entire time, reading me for cues. Then, with a shrug, he turned away. "No. No, it would not. Damn it, I'm sorry. I realise this is hard enough for you without me making it any harder." He looked at me again, the probing stare replaced by soft concern. "I'm sorry, Als. I don't know how to do this. Maybe I'm not the best person to be sharing this with," he continued when I said nothing. "You know that I, well, I also..."

"...have issues," I finished.

His laugh was short and without any humour. I noticed that his hand which held the glass was bouncing off his knee.

Jay was fumbling. Smooth Jay, always-ready-with-a-quip Jay, was at a loss for words, retreating into his shell, unsure of what to do or say. For a brief moment, I wondered if this was how Abrar felt whenever he made me feel inadequate. I ignored the twinge of guilt bubbling in my gut.

Silence sometimes does the job that words do not. As the moment stretched, it became an uncomfortable, palpable presence between us, the tension so taut that one could have reached out and plucked music from it.

I took a deep breath. I'd *chosen* to trust him at the beach because I had finally felt ready to confront my issues. He didn't ask me to do it, and I certainly didn't have to, but I did. My past, my insecurities, his issues, our complications – I would not, *could* not, let anything get the better of me.

"So, Abrar. I met him in California." I took a large swig from the drink I'd been holding for so long. "But this story starts way before that. It starts with a breakup."

ONLY THE BLIND CAN LOVE

"*That fucking bastard. That lying asshole.*"

Inaya, my bestest friend in the world, solemnly nodded and gestured to me to drink up. Not that I needed her cheering me on. I was perfectly capable of getting drunk on my own.

Because you see, today was special. I had found out that my boyfriend was cheating on me.

"I should have known." Words had a hard time making their way past my clenched teeth. My jaw hurt from the exertion.

Inaya nodded again. "You should have known."

"How did I not see this coming?"

"Oh, babe," Inaya sighed. She did it prettily like she did most things. "You saw it, alright. You just didn't *want* to see it. Let's be honest: if someone is 'really good friends' with their ex, the odds are that they are bumping uglies."

I grunted and downed another shot, unwilling to acknowledge the truth of her words. "There has to be a limit to the number of errands one could run for an ex, no?"

"Sweetie, if you're in a relationship, even a single errand for an ex is one too many." She patted my shoulder with such pity it almost disgusted me. *Almost, but not quite; part of me wanted the validation of someone acknowledging the fact that I had been wronged.*

Screwed logic, I know, but what could you do?

"You know, he kind of reminds me of my father," Inaya said.

"Who? Don't say…"

"…this waiter, you idiot, not your philandering boyfriend. Get your head out of your ass."

I didn't know whether to be angry at being called an idiot or relieved that my bestie didn't have a daddy crush on my boyfriend. I chose the easy way out; I shrugged.

"He has been doing that all evening, ever since we walked in. The way he looks at us like he doesn't approve of the choices we're making in life but he's too wise to tell us kids, not to make our own mistakes. It's very much like my dad."

I looked at Inaya, who was studying the waiter like an archaeologist as if he had just uncovered the remains of a lost ancient tomb. "You have some weird issues, my dude. And, besides," *I waved at the waiter when I saw him glancing at us again,* "he isn't the first person to disapprove of me and he certainly won't be the last. See if I give a fuck."

"I give a fuck, Alisha. Stop it!"

"You're a bitch, Ina, if you think you can dictate what I do." *The slur came not from the alcohol but the heat of my fury.* "You're important to me. But if I lean on you, you don't get to use me like a puppet. I am not your plaything. You have no right to break my trust. Do you understand?"

To her credit, Ina didn't flinch. "I understand, Ali, and I understand where this is coming from." *She touched my shoulder, then put her arm around it.* "Tell me, are you feeling better now?"

"No," *I replied and broke down for the first time that evening.* "Why does shit like this always happen to me?"

A lifetime worth of reasons had come together to fuel my reaction at that precise moment. My emotions were all a jumble. I didn't like the condescending tone she took like I was some errant child playing with the fine china at someone else's home. There was too much alcohol coursing through my blood. She sounded too much like my sister. I was tired of people treating me like an embarrassment. Could be any of them; could be all of them.

The sound of Jay clearing his throat brought me out of my reverie.

"What?" I asked.

He looked embarrassed at having caused the interruption. "Sorry, but I just want to clarify something. You're talking about Abheer here, right, and not Abrar?"

"Yes, this was Abheer," I said. "Cheating, lying Abheer who broke my heart and pushed me down the path which would end up scarring me for the rest of my life."

"Is it done?" Inaya asked me.

I took a deep breath. "Yes. I broke up with him."

"Cheers to that! So, what have you decided next?"

I noticed her voice didn't have the same tinkle over the phone. I had been noticing such things of late, small details that were easy to miss. Maybe if I had... no, I refused to walk down that dark path.

"I don't know," I replied. I honestly had no idea what I wanted to do next. "I feel like I'm done with India for now. I'm done with the *people here. Maybe I'll go abroad for a bit, take a budget trip around Europe or something for a couple of months."*

"You know, that might not be such a bad idea."

"Yeah, but I'll still have to work out the finances and stuff. I mean, even by conservative estimates, I'll spend around eighty grand on flights and another ninety on food, travel, and accommodations for a fifteen-day Euro trip. That is when I scrimp on everything."

"And I'm assuming you don't want to scrimp."

"No, goddamnit, I do not. I've done nothing but walk on eggshells these last few months with Abheer. I am not going to deny myself any longer."

"I can tell, by the speed at which you're going through guys on dating apps."

"Watch it, Ina," I warned her. "I am not in the mood for this right now."

"Woah, someone's edgy today. Sorry, girl," Inaya said. "Found anyone good?"

"Nah, most of them just want to get into my pants. And the other ones just don't want a serious relationship. I'm not in the mood for either arrangement."

"That's a good decision, Ali. I'm happy you're taking your time. The Euro trip also sounds like a good idea. Although," she hesitated as if reconsidering it.

"Out with it."

"You remember that I applied to California State University for the one-year master's program that they're offering? I just heard back from the Admissions Office. I've been accepted."

"Congratulations, babe! That's such good news. You deserve it."

"Yes, yes, thank you," she said, and I could imagine her flushing with pride. "I was thinking, why don't you apply to the course as well? It's just one year and it's a good course. And you did just say you wanted to leave India for a while."

Taken aback as I was, the idea appealed to me. One year wasn't that long, but did I really want to move abroad just to get over Abheer? "I'll think about it," I said finally.

I stopped to take a sip, only to find the glass empty. Jay took it from my hand.

"They say love is blind but, maybe, it is the other way round," I said, apropos of anything. I had to say something, anything, to fill the void that the silence had left.

"What do you mean, Als?" he said, curiosity spreadeagled over his face as he refreshed our drinks.

I shrugged. "You know, the shit people say about love being blind and stuff. I think only the blind can love – for they don't see the flaws that make us human and fallible. The rest of us just look for ways to leverage vulnerabilities for our ends."

"Such insight, much wow," he said, handing me the glass. "I'm more amazed by your reaction. You moved countries and continents to get over a broken heart. Not fond of half-measures, are you?"

His comment made me laugh which, judging by the delight on his face, was what he intended.

"Did you pour the whole freaking bottle into this one?" I winced at the strength of the drink he'd handed me. "Fuck, it's making my eyes water."

He shrugged. "You looked like you needed something stronger. It's getting intense."

"It isn't a patch on what happened next."

INAYA

I heard sounds of conversation from Inaya's room as I walked past. She must have gotten someone home last night when I was at the campus. My suspicions proved true a moment later when she walked out giggling in a hastily buttoned shirt – just the shirt, and not hers – and almost bumped into me.

"Well, you're up early today," she punched me lightly on the arm.

"And you, I'm assuming, had another late night." We walked together into the kitchen. Inaya immediately stuck her head into the fridge, while I cleaned out the filter on the coffee machine and put on some coffee to brew.

"Well, you know, I met some people. Where's the orange juice?"

"It's in there somewhere," I said as I deliberated between toast, a bowl of cereal and an omelette for breakfast. I rejected them all and started making a cheese salami sandwich. "You know, a bunch of us were talking last night about how most people who get out after a long jail sentence eat to their heart's content at the nearest diner. It's almost the first thing that they do."

"Interesting," Inaya said absently, still rummaging in the fridge for the juice. For the effort she was putting in, it might as well be a wardrobe into the land of Narnia. "This was for your podcast?"

"No, the podcast was on something else. This was just a random discussion down at the community radio station."

"Mmmhmm. And what of it?"

I poured myself a cup of coffee and took a bite of my sandwich. "And we all agreed that you could give those prisoners a lesson in indulgence."

That made her step back. "I thought we agreed on this. No slut-shaming."

Although she meant her glare to be threatening, she looked cute as a button – a half-naked button. Still, I raised my hand in a conciliatory gesture. "Sorry, sorry. It's just a remarkable turnaround for someone who was just now, judging me for talking to guys."

"Whatever, bruh. Things change, times change, people change. The only constant, or however the hell that saying goes." She hoisted the empty carafe. "And we're out of orange juice. How are we supposed to host a party tonight when we have no orange juice to go with the vodka?"

I almost choked on my sandwich. "We're hosting a party tonight?"

"Yes." She waved her hands around, carafe and all. "Jack and his dorm-mates and a few of their friends will come over. They'll get the alcohol. We need to stock up on food and mixers."

"Ina, we talked about this the last time. We have to discuss before we finalise a party."

"I know, I know, I know." She walked over to me with puppy-dog eyes. "But I really like Jack and we had a great time last night and it's still great in the morning and I think I can see something long-term here and don't you want me to be happy, Ali?"

It was hard to say no to Inaya when she turned on her charm. God, I hated how she knew she could pull shit like this off. Wishing I had her luck, I marked my protest with idle threats of bodily harm. "You manipulative bitch. I should be pouring hot coffee down your shirt."

"I love you too, Ali," she displayed her most winsome smile. "Could you also be an absolute darling and get a couple of large boxes of orange juice when you go out?"

"No. Make do with cranberry. We still have that I think. Unless one of your boy-toys has already guzzled it down."

Inaya made a face. "I hate cranberry. It tastes like paracetamol."

"Then be an absolute darling and get your own freaking orange juice," I smiled back at her. "I've got classes all day and will be busy with the podcast in the evening."

"Fine, be that way. But there are a lot of cute guys in their group and I think you could hit it off with a few of them. I know you want to make your bitch of an ex jealous."

"I don't want to."

"Right, and you stalk him on Instagram and Facebook and God knows what else just because you want to make sure he's not too broken up about the breakup," she said as she walked away. "Anyway, please try to be here around eight-ish, at the max. They'll be here early and I don't want to be the only girl around when they arrive."

※

"Are you and Inaya close?" Jay asked, abruptly, but something in his tone told me that he had been mulling it for a while.

"If only it was that simple," I sighed. "We were close during the beginning of our term at Cal State. Of course, we knew each other well even back here. Then our paths... diverged."

"Mmmhmm. I'm sensing a story within a story here."

I shook my head. "Just the usual stuff. I returned to India to attend my sister's wedding. She remained in the US to explore opportunities. The distance and time did the rest. I haven't spoken to her in over a year now."

I don't know what made me hold back from telling Jay the truth just then. Up until that moment, it had been so easy to talk to him about all of this. His companionship had made me feel comfortable enough to lay bare all the secrets I'd hidden away from the rest of the world. Maybe that was the reason I hesitated. Trust was a new commodity for me – untested, unused, unfamiliar. I did not wish to overindulge and leave myself vulnerable again.

He looked at me for a while before shrugging. "Fine, I won't prod you further. Tell me whenever you feel like you're ready to share."

"Cool." It was time to put the ball in his court again. "Why did you ask me about Inaya?"

There was a long pause. "I think, hmm..." he said at long last. I could almost see the cogs in his brains turning. "I think I might have an issue with Inaya."

"Oh, really?" This was surprising. "Why?"

"You say she was your best friend but she doesn't seem to care much about you. From whatever you've told me, the only thing that stands out is how your identity as a person interacts with her self-image. Your need for support and affection validates her. Her attention makes you feel valued and wanted. It's a classic case of co-dependent behaviour."

Taken aback by how bluntly he spoke, it took me a while to come up with a response. "I didn't know you held a PhD in human psychology."

"What? No!" He laughed. "I've just had severe and long-term practical experience. With both sides of the coin, in case you're wondering."

"No wonder you're so put together," I retorted.

Jay laughed again. "I know, right? It's a blessing, it's a curse." He topped his drink and looked at me. "You want a refill?"

I waved away his offer. I wanted to remain coherent and in control of my narrative. Jay had hit upon a raw nerve with his comment about Inaya. Questions swarmed me like angry bees. How much had I inadvertently revealed? Was it this obvious to everyone else? Did the truth always hurt so much?

The answers, I realised, didn't matter. There was nothing I could have done about them, anyway. But I needed to be more careful around Jay.

AN INCORRIGIBLE FLIRT

"*Time to bell the cat,*" Inaya plopped down next to me on the couch. I had a drink in my hand and there was a party going on in our living room. A couple was making out – I hope, just that – in the balcony. Things were just escalating without any restraint here.

"Are you finally getting married?" I asked her.

Horror and disgust battled for dominance over her features for a moment, before she composed herself. "If you think this chick is going to tie herself a knot..."

"...it'd be the sailor's knot for the noose. I know," I finished. "You know, Ina, I don't think I've ever seen someone as commitment-phobic as you."

"I know for a fact that you never will," she trilled happily, slurping on whatever alcoholic concoction had now been prepared by the bartender for the night. "There's someone who has been mooning at you through the night. I thought you should know."

I stayed silent. Inaya stayed even more silent. A simple conversation had turned into a battle of wills in a party I had never asked for. Why couldn't just people leave me be?

"Alright, fine, I'll take that bait. Who is it?" I said, eventually.

She smiled. "See, I knew you'd be interested."

"Yeah, yeah. I just want to enjoy a drink in peace without you hanging around looking at me like an expectant father."

"Noman," she said. The triumph in her voice playing its trumpets and cymbals.

I sighed. "Oh, hell no to that, sister. Nuh-uh, never, not happening at all."

"Why?" Her disbelief made me feel like I had just confessed to stepping down as the Queen of England. "He's good-looking. He is a good conversationalist. And he's interested in you."

"He's also an incorrigible flirt who's in love with the idea of romance. He just wants someone. It would hardly matter who it is, as long as there's someone."

"Hmm, maybe you're right," she gave in finally. "He did pester me for nearly two weeks to go out for dinner with him. Now, we barely talk."

I spread my hands emphatically to make my point and succeeded in knocking over Inaya's drink. The carpet's natural grey took on a much darker hue.

"We'll have to clean that up tomorrow," Inaya said.

"Exactly how I envisioned spending my Sunday," I replied bitterly. "I need another drink."

"Why were you at the party if you weren't enjoying it?" Jay asked.

"It's not like I had another option. It was happening right there, in the hall." I shut the door to the washroom for emphasis. "What was I supposed to do, lock myself up in my room?"

Jay shrugged. "I don't know. Worth a shot?"

"Not really. When these guys partied, they partied hard. A steel door in a concrete bunker wouldn't have mattered," I replied. "Are we out of alcohol?"

He looked at the near-finished bottle on the bedside table, then at the one lying empty on the floor. "I suppose we will have to raid the mini-bar, after all."

"As long as you're paying for it," I said, making myself comfortable on the bed. "When did we finish two bottles of alcohol?"

"Somewhere in between the beach and now," Jay replied, replenishing our drinks with the meagre supplies of the hotel mini-bar. "So what was the deal with Noman?"

"Inaya had taken it upon herself to find me a match. She thought I'd been repressing myself since the breakup with Abheer. According to the Gospel of Inaya, I could do well with a good date or two."

"Mmm, and she didn't think you were capable of finding a satisfactory match on your own?"

"Apparently not." I laughed. "My priorities were to study and operate my podcast. I didn't have the time to be dating, and definitely not at Inaya's speed. I told her that over and over again."

"Did she listen?"

"No," I replied with a sigh. "She carried on as if it was her divine charge to be mixed up in my business. She tried *so* hard to push me on Noman that night."

"And how did that work out?"

"Like a dream." I took a big swig of my drink. "Like a horrible, sickening, twisted dream."

THE TWISTED DREAM I

"Ooooh, looks like someone didn't need my help, after all," Inaya crooned softly behind me.

I pulled on the cigarette to hide the grin. "Shut up, Ina."

"Noman is heartbroken. He's been moping while the two of you have been busy talking the night away." She walked up to me and held out her hand for the cigarette. "What were you discussing?"

"Oh, this and that. We were discussing our countries and cultures, our habits, life here at Cal State."

"For the past four hours? Girl, you need a manual on 3 AM conversations."

I blushed despite myself. "Well, we've been talking about other stuff as well. His long-time girlfriend broke up with him right after he moved to the US. I told him a bit about Abheer."

"Opportunity, my friend, for you to swoop in." Inaya arched an eyebrow. "I have to say I quite like him. An upgrade on the option I came up with. He's got those exotic looks, that sexy accent, that dark, brooding, bad boy aura. He's the quintessential tall, dark, and handsome. Do you know he is Lebanese?"

"Is there one guy here you haven't scoped out already?" I replied. "More importantly, does Jack know?"

"Jack is last year's news, honey. I'm with Matty now, I think."

I laughed. "Your confidence is awe-inspiring."

"Hush now, Ali, and tell me all about this delightful man-cake."

The guy she was talking about had been sharing a laugh with the acting bartender for the night. He smiled at us when he saw Inaya's finger pointed at him.

"Stop being so obvious, woman," I whispered, drawing a chuckle from her. "And there's nothing more to add to what you already know about him. He's here doing his MBA."

I didn't tell Inaya that there was much more to this guy than met the eye. I didn't talk about the surprising depth which existed beneath the façade. I didn't utter a word about how his easy-going manner, his charm, his cool-guy persona hid the scars he carried – real and figurative. She wouldn't understand or, worse, care. That, for some reason, irritated me.

Inaya turned to me, her questioning gaze bearing down upon me like a thousand-watt searchlight. My feeble resistance crumbled.

"I don't know, Ina, it's weird to talk about this stuff." I tried to light another cigarette. The bloody lighter didn't work. "His ex did quite a number on him, it seems. A grade-A asshole, and a jealous bitch to boot. She sabotaged his friendships, used his insecurities to get what she wanted. At one point, he even turned to drugs and self-harm."

"No shit?"

"No shit. I've seen it. His arms are full of scars. There must be over a hundred."

Inaya whistled. "That explains why the bomber jacket hasn't come off all evening. Screwed scene."

I nodded. "Screwed, indeed. He's been avoiding relationships since."

"He's told you all this tonight?" I nodded and she whistled again. "That's some speed. This is sixth-date stuff. You open up to people emotionally after you sleep with them, not before."

"That's just it, Ina. He's different from the other boys. He doesn't want to sleep with me. He isn't professing undying love or asking for my hand in marriage. We're just talking, you know, just getting to know each other and laying bare our souls, our hurts, our scars." I didn't know how to articulate why I felt so strongly about a guy I had just met. "Companionship, that's what he says he desires. He wants to surround himself with good people and just heal the wounds of his past. And I think he's comfortable with me."

"And you, what are you thinking?"

"I honestly don't know. I don't want a long-term romance right now, but there's a real connection here. And at least he's honest about his issues, screwed up as they are. I like him."

"Be careful, Ali. Don't make him your project. You can't heal yourself by fixing someone else." Inaya had a faraway look in her eyes. "What's his name?"

"Abrar."

"So, finally," Jay said. "Abrar."

I nodded. "Finally."

"We can stop if you want."

"No, we can't." I needed to see this through. A door had been opened and it could not be closed. "We must finish this now, for better or for worse."

I felt the earth tremble and opened my eyes in a panic – only to be greeted by the vision of Inaya standing over me, smiling sweetly, shaking me by my shoulder.

"Wake up, sleepyhead. It's almost 9 o'clock. We'll be late for the morning lectures."

"Go away, Ina," I mumbled, pulling the cover over my face. "I haven't caught a wink all night. My body needs its beauty sleep."

"Ooooooh, someone was up the whole night!" She exclaimed. "I'm assuming with the Lebanese hunk. Did you guys do the dirty?"

"Get your head out of the gutter," I could feel the alcohol from last night still coursing through my veins. "We just talked."

Inaya touched my forehead with concern. "Are you hungover? Do you have a headache?"

"No, I think I'm still drunk." I opened my unwilling eyes to face the world. Everything – the fan overhead, my bookshelf, the door to my room, Inaya's face – appeared rimmed by a light pink haze. "Ugh. I'm going to skip classes today."

"And meet your new squeeze?" She chuckled. "I think that's a marvellous plan."

I hadn't planned on doing anything today, except sleep. But meeting Abrar didn't seem like a bad idea, either.

"Well, since you're not going, I'm going to rush." Inaya got up, then hesitated. "Just make sure you shuttle Noman out by the time I return. I don't have nearly enough alcohol in the apartment to deal with his moping today."

Now it was my turn to be shocked. "He's still here?"

"Yes," she replied, standing at the door. "You should have seen how terrible he looked last night. I was only... comforting him."

"Comforting, right." I chuckled. "I'm sure he appreciated your generosity."

"Hey, no judgements, bitch. I'll be back by 5. Make sure he leaves by then."

※

"Yeah, I steadily feel less and less enamoured by Inaya. Why were you even friends?"

"Is that really your concern, Jay?"

The unexpected heat of my words brought him up short. I almost could see the cogs of his brain moving, evaluating this unexpected development, trying to come up with a response.

"Listen, Als..."

I held up a hand. "No, Jay, let it be. People have judged the choices I've made my entire life. You're not the first or the last. I just have one request."

"Anything, Alisha."

"No more interruptions, please."

※

"No, Noman. Please, stop embarrassing yourself and leave," I said as I slammed the door shut in his face.

He was dawdling there. I could feel it. What if he knocked again? Would I open the door and confront him or ignore him? I was rooted in the place.

The sound of my phone's notification broke my indecisive train of thought. Abrar had texted me.

```
Hey beautiful, what say we meet for coffee today
on campus?

I'll meet you at your place in 10 mins.
```

I texted back.

My mind made, I stepped out into the corridor. Noman was nowhere to be seen. This was just as well. I hoped he was not skulking, waiting to corner me again. I didn't know what I would do if that happened.

Thankfully, despite my apprehension, the short trip passed completely unmarked. I knocked on Abrar's door. The smile on his face was a far cry from my dark mood.

"Why can't men take no for an answer?" I pushed past him and stormed into the room. "Why do things always have to be their way?"

"What happened?" Abrar asked. He was confused. People didn't expect others to come rushing in with a full head of steam.

"There's this guy, Noman, a friend of Inaya. I met him at the party last week. He's been pestering me since."

"Noman? Noman Salah?"

"Yes. He's been texting me at odd hours, telling me how he wanted to take me out for drinks. I kept saying no. Then, today..." I suppressed an inadvertent shiver.

"What did he do?"

"He had stayed over with Inaya last night. When she left for class, he came into my room and struck up a random conversation. He started talking about me, how grateful he is to have met me and all that. He said he found me beautiful and wanted to take me out." I sat down on the bed. "I said no and told him to leave many times, but he kept flirting with me."

Abrar's face darkened. "You should not have engaged with him. You should never engage with men like him."

"I know, I know." I was surprised at how guilty his statement made me feel. "It was harmless, initially. But, as the conversation progressed, I was less and less comfortable. Next thing I know, he was sitting on the bed, touching my hair, complimenting me, getting closer."

"Why didn't you throw him out?"

The change in his tone shocked me. It turned primal, throatier, like the growl of a predator warning others to stay off his territory. "Why didn't you slap him? Do something, anything?"

"It's not like I didn't want to." I sounded more defensive than I meant to. "My body froze up. I was only shocked into action when he tried to kiss me. That's when I told him to leave."

"You should never allow other men to get so close to you."

My heart skipped a beat when I caught his glare. Those eyes held the promise of something darker, more malevolent than the charming, suave Abrar I had seen so far. I flinched involuntarily when he stood up and took out his phone. His every action carried the threat of unimaginable violence.

Before I knew it, he had called up Noman. Of course, they knew each other, two Arabic guys here at the campus. There was a lot of shouting that I didn't understand. Abrar had punched the wall twice. He turned after hanging up the phone.

"Noman will not be bothering you anymore," he said, walking towards me. "But you really should not let other men get so close to you."

I nodded meekly. Abrar stopped when he reached the bed, looming over me. "You'll learn to behave, Alisha. I'll teach you how to behave."

He leaned in and his open palm caught me full in the waist.

"That's when he assaulted me for the first time," I mumbled, staring at the empty glass in my hand. "He beat me so hard that I lost consciousness. Then he woke me up and fixed up my bruises. He told me how he was saving me from myself by teaching me to be obedient like any woman should be with her man, and why it isn't a good idea to hang out with other men. For someone else's crime, he thought it was fair to punish *me* and beat me black and blue."

"And this was when you'd barely been dating a week." Jay slumped in the chair, shook his head. "What a monster, what a fucking monster."

I laughed bitterly. "Oh, it wasn't all bad, you know, because he loved me. He told me that after he was done. How this was his way of sharing the pain and love that he felt for me."

"Why did you stay with him, Als? Why didn't you tell anyone? He should have gone to prison, where he belonged."

"Who was I going to tell, Jay, when *I* couldn't believe what had happened to me? He used everything he knew – my insecurities, my secrets, my flaws – to completely erode my sense of self." Tears ran down in torrents, unwilling to be held back any longer. "I remember when Inaya confronted him about this... incident. Most of his friends were there, amongst other people we both knew. She had chosen her moment well."

"Do you know what he did? He *apologised*. For being emotionally damaged, for being unaware of his trauma being triggered by the episode. He sat there and cried and apologised to me for all of it. The complete narrative had flipped, just like that. I ended up consoling him and telling him that I loved him, and he thanked me for being his saviour."

For a long, long, time after that, nothing moved. Nobody spoke. The silence between us was like an ancient leviathan, a menacing, slumbering presence that swallowed eternities and universes.

"You know, I have to give him this; he could be unpredictable. Once, I sent Abheer some pictures of us. He called me up immediately. It was late at night. Abrar asked me who it was. I was so scared of telling him the truth, after how he reacted when Noman proposed to me. What would he do if he knew I'd texted my ex?"

Words were the torrent now. I could not have stopped even if I wanted to – and I was tired of holding this particular dam in.

"You know what he did when I finally told him? He just laughed and clicked a few more. When he was not torturing me, he made me feel like I was the most important aspect of his life. Everything he did, good or bad, was for me, because of me."

"Where was Inaya when all of this was happening?" I could see the helplessness on Jay's face. It reminded me of how weak I used to feel back then. "Where was Alec?"

"Inaya and I had a nasty fight. She said some mean things about Abrar. I just packed my bags and moved in with Abrar. It didn't even bother her that I wasn't around. She just continued partying as she had been." I cleaned my nose into a tissue. "Alec was not around for the first month or so. He'd gone to Scotland with his family. His grandfather had passed away."

"Not that he did much when he came back," I said in a voice barely louder than a whisper. "Jay, could you turn down the AC? I've got goose-bumps all over my arms."

He didn't say a word for some time, didn't move. When he finally replied, concern tinged his voice. "Als, the AC hasn't been on for over an hour."

THE TWISTED DREAM II

I stepped out of the room to find Abrar and Alec playing NBA Online on their phones. I doubted they had moved from their positions for the past five hours.

"Abrar," I said, "I've been calling you."

"And I've been calling back, Alisha, asking why you have your knickers in a twist."

"I didn't hear anything, honey."

"Not my problem, honey."

"I've got to go down to the radio station." I tried to keep the sarcasm out of my tone. There was no telling what would trigger Abrar's rage.

That had his attention. He put his game on pause and turned to face me. "What for?"

"Sam called me up. Samantha," I clarified quickly. "She called up to check if I'm okay."

"Of course you're okay. Why can't this Sam mind her own business?"

I kept my bubbling anger in check. Patience, I reminded myself, that was the key to making this work. "I've missed many recent recording sessions, Abrar. I haven't been to any of my classes in the last two weeks. It is natural for anyone to be concerned."

"Tell her you're with me. Tell her you're absolutely fine."

"I did. That's not the only thing we discussed. She wanted me to lead a podcast featuring minority students. It's brilliant. I want to be a part of it."

"And that's decided, is it?" Abrar's voice was a little more than a husky whisper. It felt like the temperature of the room had dropped several degrees.

Alec got up. He had a nose for identifying the red flags of our arguments. "I'm going to the kitchen to get a beer. Do you want one?"

"No, I'll finish dealing with Alisha first," Abrar replied. "I told you, no more podcasts. No more hanging out with those losers from the station. You're happy here."

"But I'm not, Abrar," I spoke more forcefully than I meant to. "I don't have any friends because I don't talk to anyone anymore. I haven't attended my classes in a while. God, I haven't even spoken to Inaya in a while. I miss her stupid parties. I don't live. I exist."

"You're not happy." I hated how he made it sound like an indictment. The sound of Alec's door shutting seemed like a fitting counterpoint to his statement.

"I mean, I'm happy when I'm with you. But when you're busy doing your stuff, I am bored out of my mind. I need to live my own life, Abrar, so that we can bring even more happiness to each other."

He loomed over me, like the Colossus of Rhodes over a puny mortal. Then he smiled, and it was like the sun had broken through the clouds again.

"Of course, you're right, babe. I've been so focused on my healing that I've ignored your needs. I'm sorry." He held my hand. "You go on ahead to the radio station. I'll get us some wine and cook your favourite gyros. When you come back, we'll have a romantic candlelit dinner right here. And then, if you're in the mood, maybe some Netflix and chill with less Netflix, more chill?"

I laughed. A weight I wasn't aware I was carrying suddenly lifted from my shoulders. "You're a dog, Abrar." *I leaned forward on my toes and kissed him.* "I love you."

"I love you so much, baby."

***

"That's... some anti-climax. I could have sworn something bad was about to happen," Jay said. "I didn't realise I had been holding my breath this entire time."

"I told you, he was like that a lot. One moment he was a monster, the next he could be the most caring person in the world."

"That sounds like a horrible, horrible place to be in."

"No shit, Sherlock," I laughed. The sound had no mirth, no joy – just the deep anguish of a creature hurting from an old, unhealed wound. "Can you imagine, though, what that kind of switch does to another person?"

Jay shook his head.

"I'll tell you, Jay. It completely strips away your sense of self. You're not sure of your feelings. Your abuser becomes your primary source of attention and validation. You make excuses on their behalf, and you alienate yourself from everyone who doesn't feel that way. He used to hold me after assaulting me, crying in my arms, apologising to me, telling me how much he loved me, thanking me for saving his soul, asking me if I loved him. And I always, always said yes."

"There were times when I argued with myself that what he did to me, what he was doing to me, wasn't horrendous – even as it was happening for the umpteenth time. And you should have heard some of the excuses I made on his behalf. His ex had scarred him too deeply. He was a complex, complicated man."

And, just like that, it was gone. The flickering light of the raw, emotional, broken individual underneath Jay's suavity and humour had disappeared, leaving in its wake familiar traits – the composure, the analytical gaze that took in everything and revealed nothing. I sighed. There were no mutually cathartic moments like they show in the movies, where two people just bare their true selves to each other throughout a conversation. Life could never be that straightforward.

"There's not much else to tell. Or, rather, it's too much of the same patterns repeating themselves over and over again. Abuse, apologise, care, repeat. Looking back at it, I think I'd become numb to it all after a point. The drugs had helped."

"What?!"

I chuckled. "Oh, yeah! That dinner he promised, remember? He made me have some of his magic pills, for the first time. For the entire week after, he treated me like a princess – getting me my morning coffee, preparing all the meals, spending all of his time with me. He didn't even play that stupid game that he and Alec spent hours on. All so he could get me addicted and keep me docile."

"How did you finally break free from his clutches?"

And, just like that, it was my turn to take a deep breath. "It took impending death for me to break free. That, and a rude awakening."

I woke up with a heavy head. My mouth was drier than a desert. I didn't recollect much of what happened last night – bare snatches of images and sounds. I was in the bathroom, naked. There was a half-eaten slice of bread near me.

"Come out, Alisha." *Abrar pounded on the door. I was hit by a sense of déjà vu.* "It's time for lunch."

I had gooseflesh all over my body. All I could remember was feeling scared and angry and confused – and afraid for my life.

"No, I won't," *I replied.* "You'll kill me."

He laughs. "Are you crazy? Why on earth would I kill you? I love you."

"No, you're lying. You're upset with me. You're upset with something I've done."

"Babe, we've both been upset with each other before and we're both still breathing," *Abrar cooed on the other side of the door.* "Come on, now. Open the door. This has gone on long enough."

The logic was sound, convincing. Like any other couple, Abrar and I had fought before. We had always come out stronger. And yet, despite his feather-soft tone, I couldn't shake the feeling that something was different this time. For one thing, I could imagine no reason why I'd locked myself up in the bathroom. I also didn't remember being this afraid for my life, ever before.

"You said... you said you will kill me." *More snatches of the past came back to me.* "You got angry because I wouldn't open the bathroom door."

And, just like that, it all came back to me. It started innocuously. It always started innocuously. Any little thing – like interrupting him when he played NBA Online, or speaking my mind, or wanting to meet a friend, or just not responding as he desired – could trigger his rage.

Yesterday, it was because I had refused his request to bathe together. He shouted and raged and kicked the door before locking me up and leaving to god-knows-where for hours. He slid in a slice of bread under the door sometime late at night. I'd eaten as much as I could before my mouth dried up.

"What I said then was just in the heat of the moment, Alisha. I say 'screw you' in anger to Alec several times a day. Do you think I have any intention of actually doing that to him?"

Last night's dinner had ants crawling all over it. "I'm not opening the door, Abrar."

There was silence outside for a moment. "Fine, stay in the damned bathroom," *he said.* "Stay and starve, for all I care. Let me make sure you stay there." *The gentle, indulgent cajoling of his tone was replaced by a gruff indifference. I heard the key turning in the lock.* "There, suit yourself."

I didn't hear him saying 'bitch' but I could sense, from the sound of the door slamming out in the hall, that he was not pleased.

"Wow," Jay said. "Just wow. When did he finally let you out?"

"He didn't," I replied. Exhaustion swept over me, making me regret drinking so much. "Inaya did."

"Fuck." Jay exhales noisily. "That's quite a story."

"To you, maybe," I replied, no longer bothering to hide the quaver in my voice. "To me, it's a reality I've lived through. Every day is a fight to suppress it."

I wondered idly how many days I would spend before exhaustion, hunger, and stress killed me. Will anyone even miss me if I was dead? Had they even noticed my absence? Probably not.

I heard loud voices out in the room, getting louder. I got up and put my ear against the door and caught snatches of the conversation.

"...not done, Abrar. Her parents called me up to ask why she isn't picking up her phone. Where have you kept her?"

I banged my fists against the door and shouted as hard as I could. A minute later, the door opened. It was Inaya. My friend, Inaya, who I fought with over this monster standing behind her. I was so relieved I started crying.

"Oh, Ina," I said between sobs. Tears flowed thick and fast. "I'm so glad you came to me. I'm sorry I ever left you. I'm sorry we fought. I promise I'll never fight with you again."

Inaya glared at Abrar, who didn't even have the decency to look guilty. "You kept her locked up in the bathroom, you crazy idiot? Did you even give her anything to eat? Alec, could you get her something to eat?"

Alec, who had been standing at the entrance to the room, nodded and walked toward the kitchen. I didn't want him to go. I wanted as many people as possible between me and Abrar.

"I don't care about any of that, Ina. Let's go. Let's just go." *I tugged at her sleeve.* "I don't want to stay here anymore. Please, let's leave."

"You're not going anywhere, Alisha," *Abrar growled and took a step towards me. When I flinched involuntarily, his bearing changed.* "Listen, babe. This was all just a misunderstanding, right? I overreacted. I'm sorry. We'll work this out, I promise. You know I love you."

"Let her leave, Abrar." *Alec was back with some toast and fruit juice. Unable to stand the sight of bread, I broke down in Inaya's arms.* "I know you've been dosing her with your drugs. End this, right now, or I'll be forced to involve others."

For a heart-stopping moment, it seemed as if Abrar might attack him. Though they were the same height, Alec could not have overpowered Abrar. As for me and Inaya... I couldn't even bear thinking about it.

Abrar spit on the floor and turned away from us. "Screw you all. I don't need any of you. Take that bitch and leave. As far as I'm concerned, it's good riddance."

I stood silent.

"Als?"

"Inaya went back to Abrar's after getting me back to our place to get some of my stuff."

"And that was that?" Jay asked.

"No. She didn't return for a long, long time. I was scared that Abrar might have hurt her for taking me away. When I finally drummed up the courage to check up after her, I saw Alec standing outside in the corridor."

"Alec?"

"Yes, Alec. Sweet, non-confrontational, well-meaning Alec." Unloading this burden was supposed to make me feel lighter and better. All I felt was tiredness beyond measures, deep exhaustion of the soul. "He wanted to apologise to me for not stepping in sooner. He didn't want to interfere, he said because he knew Abrar was a complex person and I didn't seem to mind his bipolar behaviour. He didn't want to complicate the situation."

"And Inaya?"

Inaya. The knife that had cut the deepest. "When I returned to Abrar's, Alec asked me not to go inside. He said... he said I wouldn't like what I saw. He was right. When I stepped in, she and Abrar were.." The recollection was so painful I wanted to curl up and cry. I wondered how I kept myself together back then. Maybe I was just too numbed by everything. "In a flash, it all became clearer. When he left me the previous day, he'd gone to her. All those late-night texts with his cousins in Lebanon, they were from her."

Jay sat beside me and put his arm around me. "I'm so sorry, Als," he whispered.

"It was a long time ago," I said, even though the pain was still as fresh as the day I'd been hurt - first by the man I'd loved, then by the friend I'd trusted. "Jay, I'm really tired."

"Come here," Jay snuggled me in his embrace.

I closed my eyes and put my head on his chest. Before I could notice, I passed into the realm of slumber.

THE REASON IS YOU

Jay was snoring when I woke up, his arm slung around my waist. I didn't mind it. A lot of things had changed last night. I spent several minutes running over the chain of events, of what I'd revealed to him. The thought of being emotionally vulnerable around him did not make me feel weak. It had felt good to be heard and understood. I realised I wanted this. I had wanted this for a long time to come.

I tried to disengage his arm as unobtrusively as I could to get my morning coffee. Jay still woke up, groaning loudly.

"Good morning, sleepyhead," I said. "Want some coffee?"

"Some poison would be better. I haven't had a hangover this bad since forever." He groaned again. "You know, I'll take you up on that coffee. Black as sin, no sugar, and some lime."

"Is this your go-to cure for hangovers?" I asked as I put the kettle to boil.

"This is my go-to cure for life," he replied. "What's got you smiling so wide? You look as if you have a hangar in your mouth."

I was not surprised. I was feeling something close to happiness. For the first time in God knows how long, I wasn't lonely.

"Well, I'm in a good mood," I said. "And, as Hoobastank said it, the reason is you."

Jay shrugged. "I did nothing, Alisha. I just sat there and listened to the horrors you've gone through."

"Are you kidding me?" I handed him his coffee and sat down next to him. "Do you know how rare an experience that is for me? Most people in my life don't listen to me, Jay, and I don't share any of the stuff that matters, anyway. I could connect with you on a level that I haven't done with anyone before. Not even with Inaya, who was my best friend since we were little runts in kindergarten. To open your soul to someone like that, it's an exhilarating, frightening feeling.

"The fear is mine, and mine alone. I've been hurt too many times to not be afraid of being vulnerable. But, when I'm with you, it doesn't matter. I feel whole, complete, like a part of me that I didn't know was missing is put back together. Remember what you said about people having jagged edges? Yours don't cut me, Jay. My heart doesn't bleed as much when I'm with you. Your broken complements mine."

The sound of life trickled in through the balcony, carrying the indistinct murmur of the city waking up from its half-slumber. Car horns honked out in the street, interspersed with the babble of the crowds moving to their destinations. The morning brought with it a sense of hope, of a fresh beginning. I couldn't help but notice the curious counterpoint it presented to how I felt last night at the beach. Not that I was complaining; I simply breathed it all in.

Jay hadn't replied, so I continued. "This feeling, it's a salve to my soul. It makes me want to be more than I was, to be better than I was before. People say that you don't fall in love – you rise. I think I understand what that means, now. I want to give us a chance, Jay. I want to share with you the happiness that I feel right now." I laughed, a nervous giddiness stealing over me. "Just one day at a time, you know. We can make each other happy for just one day, and see if we can keep doing that for the rest of our lives."

Silence followed my sudden proclamation of love. Our coffees cooled in it.

"Alisha," Jay said. "I don't know what to say."

That was not the response I had expected. "Something along the lines of 'that sounds like a good idea' would be nice," I muttered.

Jay simply shook his head. "Thank you for the faith you place in me, Alisha, but I can't do this."

"Do what?"

"This. Us." He gestured with his hands. He was sitting with his back to the wall, his features flicking through a multitude of emotions. "Trust me, Alisha, I would have liked nothing better. I find you witty, and intelligent, and sometimes inadvertently funny. We share a companionship that most people can only dream of. The easiest thing to do is to say yes to you."

"Then why don't you?" Questions swirled in my mind like a raging torrent, the hopes and dreams of just a moment ago vanishing like breath upon a mirror. Jay frequently talked about how much he cared about me, how deeply he felt for me. Now that I was beginning to feel for him the same way, why did he hesitate? Were all those broad claims just meaningless posturing? To what end?

"Because, sometimes, going downhill is easier than climbing up. I have a saviour complex, Alisha. I am attracted to broken things and impossible situations. I've worked so hard to overcome it. If I give in to this, right now, I will risk unravelling everything." He looked up at me, then, with those knowing eyes that had dissected and diagnosed everything that wouldn't work with us. Why, oh why, couldn't they reflect what was in my heart? "I can't – won't – make you my next project. I will not fall back to my old patterns again. I don't want to cause any more pain to either you or me."

"And what of the pain I feel right now, Jay?"

He closed his eyes and took a deep breath. "Sometimes, Als, it's better to hurt a little now to avoid getting hurt more in the future."

Heartbroken as I was, I felt a strange relief upon hearing those words. This was familiar territory. I was used to rejection. People didn't reciprocate what I felt. They broke my trust. Jay was neither the first nor the last to do so.

With that realisation came anger. "Then where do we go from here, Jay? To just being friends? Because this sure as hell isn't like any friendship that I know of. We were cuddling just this morning, for heaven's sake. We're both attracted to each other. Who's to say that, some other night, a similar scene won't lead to it? What will we do then? Will it make you slip back into your old patterns again? Will you then give this a shot?"

Jay looked like he wanted to respond, but I held up my hand. I didn't want him to give me any more explanations. "You know what, let it be. Forget I ever said anything to you. I'll finish whatever is left of our project here. Then I'm going back to Delhi." Anger helped me cut through the confusion. I wanted to end my professional dependency on him. I would ask my dad for seed capital and start my own business. "Goodbye, Jay. I'd appreciate it if you could close the door on your way out."

CROSSING OCEANS

"How did your pitch go, yesterday?" My dad asked. I was sitting with him and my mother at the table for breakfast.

I pushed around some food on the plate. "It went well."

"And you're confident that you'll close the account?"

"I suppose," I replied.

He put down the newspaper he had been reading. "You should be happy, *beta*. You've done well to build a business up from scratch. You've built your reputation in your field. Top brands are reaching out *to* you, instead of the other way round. What bothers you still?"

"It's that boy, Jay," Mum chimed in on my behalf. "She's still sulking because of him."

"Mom, enough! This is not about Jay."

"It's already been months, Alisha. You need to move on." My mother's persistence knew no bounds; terriers could have taken lessons on doggedness from her. It was an irritating attribute, especially combined with her complete lack of tact.

My phone's email notification rang before I could blow my top. Dad swooped in to save the day.

"Maybe it's those people from Darron Inc. Maybe they've sent you a contract."

I looked at my phone, aghast. It wasn't Darron. It was the last person I had expected an email from.

As I twisted and turned in my bed for the thousandth time that night, I checked the email again. It was still there. I didn't know whether I expected it to magically disappear, or just thought of it as part of an extended nightmare.

Hey, Alisha, it read. How have you been? It's been a long time and I really, really miss you. We never even got to say goodbye when you left. My fault, I suppose. I was a complete ass to you during the last few months.

That, I felt, was a massive understatement. This person had ripped my heart out and trampled it into the dust. And now, out of the blue, an email that goes on as if nothing ever changed between us.

I do hope you're doing well, Ali, and I'm sorry for whatever I did to you. Is it too late to tell you that I regret spreading those malicious rumours about you? I suppose it is.

I don't even know why I'm writing this email to you right now. What am I looking for? Forgiveness? Redemption? Someone who could understand what I'm going through right now? These things are beyond me, anyway. I burnt my bridges when I betrayed my best friend. It is only fitting that I pay the price for it. Karma is a bitch.

Anyway, enough about me. I saw someone tag you on a post somewhere. You're running a business? Finally! That's wonderful. I am happy for you. You finally found the thing to call your own. I hope that life showers you with all the success and happiness that you deserve.

Goodbye, Ali. May we meet again, in a better world. Hope you forgive me.

With all my love,

Your once-friend,

Inaya

It hit me in my guts. I was happy to hear from her but what did she mean she was paying for her wrongdoings? The contents of the letter seared a grave image on my mind. I couldn't shake the feeling that Inaya's life was in danger – the same feeling I had when Abrar had locked me up in the bathroom. Was he doing to her what he had done to me?

She deserves it, a part of me whispered back. *She said so herself. She chose this monster over you. She worked with him to destroy your confidence, your sense of worth, your reputation. She deserves all this and more.*

And yet, part of me couldn't help but feel like I was meant to save her from the hell I knew all too well. Sleep passed me by that night, as the devil and the angel fought to assert their dominance.

"Dad, I'm liquidating the business."

"What?!" He and Mum said at the same time. While my mother spluttered, my dad recovered quickly. "But you're doing so well, Alisha. Why do you want to stop it now?"

"I have to, dad. There's someone in trouble and I have to help her."

"There you go again, throwing away everything on a whim," my mother lamented. "You always do this. Always." She pointed a finger at my father. "Didn't I tell you she'd do this?"

Seeing my expression, dad tried to diffuse the situation. "This is not the time or place, darling." He turned to me. "Listen, *beta*, is it necessary to do this?"

His question made me think. Did I have to do this? I would've done anything for Inaya at one point of time. She had also hurt me, deeply, to the core. It had taken a lot of painstaking effort to rebuild my life after she and Abrar had tried to sabotage it. Was I okay with throwing it all away on a whim, for a person who had put me through so much?

But, I realised, saving her from Abrar was not about her. To me, it was a way to bury my demons, to heal the scars that I carried. So, yes, I had to do it – for no one else but me.

"Yes, dad ," I replied. "It's the only way."

As I waited for the plane to take off, I couldn't help but reflect on what had followed. My mother had cribbed, as usual, unleashing a well-rehearsed tirade about me and my life choices. I had ignored her. It was more difficult to deal with dad's silent disappointment. While he immediately called up his legal advisor to initiate the dissolution of the business, I couldn't help but feel he disapproved of my decision to give up everything I'd built and go chasing wild hunches.

I had tried explaining why doing this was important to me. Inaya was in trouble. Regardless of our past, I had to save her. More importantly, I had to save myself. I'd carried the invisible mark of trauma for so many years now. This act felt like life coming full circle. It was a chance for me to undo, at least in some small measure, what had been done to me back then.

Maybe it made sense to them, maybe it didn't. I didn't have the luxury to sit and deliberate.

During the layover in London, I dropped Alec a text. His reply only made it across after I landed in the US. He told me he would be waiting for me at the airport to pick me up. True to his word, he was there. As we drove to his place, we caught up with the latest developments in each other's life. He told me about how he got into a relationship and out of it within a few months because his ex-girlfriend was incredibly anal about everything. I told him about Jay, how we'd drifted apart after he turned me down, and the new business I'd set up.

"That's great news, Alisha," Alec said. "I always knew you'd do well for yourself. You were a bright star, even on campus."

"Yeah, it's all been a stroll in the park," I replied. "I've asked my dad to close my business."

Alec looked stunned. "Why?"

"I need to find Inaya and Abrar. I have a feeling that Inaya is in trouble, Alec. Big trouble. We need to help her out. We need to get Abrar behind bars."

I told him everything that had happened in the last few days – Inaya's email out of the blue, my decision to come to the US to find her, the liquidation of my business.

"Alisha, it feels like a crusade." He pulled into the driveway of his house. "The last I saw them, Inaya and Abrar were happy with each other."

"You also thought I was happy with Abrar, and you were practically living with us then. How long has it been since you saw them, anyway?" I tried – and failed – to keep the bitterness out of my tone. "Do you feel you can afford to be wrong again?"

Alec was silent for a moment. "I can't apologise enough for that, Alisha. I'm sorry you went through what you did. I can't tell you how much I regret not stepping in earlier. But this..."

"I don't need your sympathy, Alec, or your apologies. They can't change what happened. You know it as well as I do that, sooner or later, Abrar will revert to type. I need your help to protect Inaya from that. I *want* you, my best friend, to be there with me when I face the demons of my past." I stepped out of the car. "It's okay if you're not in this, you know. I'll manage it. I just want you to be here."

His gaze alternated between the sky, me and my luggage. "Screw it," he said finally. "I'll help you, Alisha. Even if I have to move mountains, I'll help you find Abrar."

FORREST

"So, you're saying this man abused and tortured you, and you had evidence of it that has since been deleted, and now you want us to find and arrest this person because you *think* he's doing the same thing to your friend – the one who went with him after knowing everything he did to you?" The cop tapped his pen on the blank notepad in front of him. "Do you see why that chain of events would be an issue for any law enforcement official?"

The way he said it made the entire thing feel ridiculous – and this was when I'd lived through it. To anyone who hadn't been a part of it, what I said would have appeared like a gross exaggeration, at best, and an outright fabrication at worst.

I looked around the police station. Regardless of which part of the globe it was, a police station was an all-too-familiar sight. Bored cops with weather-beaten faces and greyed hair hung around the water cooler and coffee dispenser, sharing details about their latest case. Some shuffled along files that had nowhere important to be, with no particular sense of urgency. There was a loud commotion somewhere inside the building, the sounds of shouting and cursing. These were people who had seen it all, who continuously came up against the worst that humanity had to offer – whether amongst their colleagues or amongst the criminals they faced.

"Alec, this is hopeless," I said with a sinking feeling in the pit of my stomach. I could sense that these people would not help us. "Let's go."

Alec, to his credit, did not give up without a fight. "But there *must* be something you can do to help, officer. Isn't there any alternative recourse available to us?"

A door was shut with a force strong enough to echo across the entire precinct.

"And you can tell the Chief to suck it, too, Walter," a wiry, middle-aged person shouted as he stormed out of the building.

"Well, there goes your alternative recourse," the cop said to us. "That guy's name is Forrest. He was the top detective at this precinct. If anyone could help you, he would."

"Thank you," Alec said and looked at me with relief. "Thank you so much."

"Don't thank me yet." The cop gathered his papers. "That one has a mean temper on him. And, judging by his mood, he's just been fired by the captain. I wouldn't want to cross his path just yet."

We rushed out and caught up with Detective Forrest smoking just outside.

"Detective Forrest?" I said.

"Just Forrest now, missy. I am not a detective anymore. Not that it matters in this dump." He gestured towards the precinct. "There are people with badges in there who ought to be locked up with the criminals that they catch. Not a half-decent policeman amongst that lot."

"We need your help," Alec interrupted him.

"Did you hear a word I just said, sonny?" Forrest turns his piercing gaze at Alec. "I'm not a detective."

"That's good," I said, "because a detective can't help us in our case."

We were sitting in Forrest's house out in the suburbs. It was a lonely place, cluttered and messy. There was no one around, even though the shelf held some pictures of what I assumed were family members.

"Tell me about this guy again," Forrest said, pouring himself another glass of whiskey. Alec and I had turned down his offer of drinks. "Everything you can remember."

And so I told him about Abrar, about Inaya, about how things had panned out between us. He asked questions from time to time to clarify some minor details – his height, his face, his temperament – before turning to Alec. He asked him about his time with Abrar, how they became friends, whether he knew the stuff he was up to. Alec answered all of his questions, as truthfully as he could.

At the end of the interview, Forrest leaned back and whistled. "Quite a nasty piece of work, this fellow. And you deleted all the incriminating evidence." He wagged his finger at me. "God forbid it ever happens to you again, missy. Always keep the dirt you have on people. You never know when you might need it."

"Will you help us or not?"

"Help you? Hell, yes," he replied. "I'd love to put this bastard behind bars. But we need a plan. So here's what we're going to do."

BLACK AS SIN

"We're getting nowhere with this, Alec," I said, throwing another wasted lead into the trash can. We had been searching for Abrar and Inaya for three days. Forrest had gone to speak with some of his contacts in the California Department of Corrections and Rehabilitation to see if anyone who matched Abrar's description had been processed by them. It was a long shot, but all we had were long shots.

"We'll find him, don't worry," Alec replied, leaning back in his chair. "You just need some fresh air. Come, let's get some coffee."

"How is coffee going to help here?"

"It's better than sitting around and moping," he quipped.

I was reluctant to leave. There was just so much that needed to be done. But Alec's advice made sense. We weren't getting anything else accomplished.

"Fine," I said, getting up from my perch on the bed. "But you're buying."

We walked down the short distance to the nearest Starbucks and grabbed a table. Alec got our orders – a Latte for me, and an Americano for himself.

"Ummm, just how I like it." He took a tentative sip. "Black as sin, with no sugar."

That statement took me back to a time when things looked hopeful, for once. "Jay drank his coffee like that."

Alec looked at me from the top of his cup. "You know, Alisha, you've never given me the dirt on Jay."

"There's not much to tell, man," I said as he made a face. "Just that the next time I'm opening up to someone, it'll be my autopsy."

I hadn't spoken to Jay since that night. I'd spoken *about* him even less. At that moment, as hard as I tried, the right words didn't come to me. What *was* Jay to me? Just someone who, in a short span, had become one of the most important people in my life. Just a friend I wanted more of and got even less. "We hung out as friends for a while, even worked together. We were close, you know. He got me on a level that no one else did. I was comfortable around him. Less edgy, I suppose, more relaxed in my skin."

"So, what happened?"

I sighed. "I opened up to him about Abrar, about everything. I thought that we were reaching a place where we could look at something more than friendship. He didn't agree. I suppose he didn't want to bleed on my jagged edges."

"What?"

"Just something he used to say. That we're all broken people, looking for others who match our broken. We cut each other when the pieces don't fit."

"Ooof! Your boy sounds like a philosopher," Alec said.

"He could say something almost wise from time to time," I replied with a wry half-smile.

"I warned you not to get too close to him. The guys that you fall for inevitably end up hurting you."

"It was not his fault, Alec. I wanted to take our situations a bit further. He turned me down. So I did what I knew best: burned my bridges and cut him out of my life. We haven't talked since."

"Such healthy behaviour. Glad to know you haven't changed." When I punched him on the arm, he smiled. "Finish your coffee. I know exactly how to cheer you up." He always knew how to cheer me up. Despite being head over heels for Jay, Alec was still irreplaceable in my life. He did bail out at first when I needed him, but he has always been there for me ever since. I may have opened up my wounds far more easily to Jay because of the absolute disconnect he shared with my past. But my heart knew who had listened to it grieve over and over again. It knew that had it not been for Alec, Jay would never have met the stronger, more stable version of me. Alec had given me the courage to love again, which was what made him irreplaceable.

"You know, I don't think that eating a Sub in India compares with eating it here," I said with a mouthful of sandwich. "I missed this."

"I missed you," Alec said, his hand resting on mine. He gave it a little squeeze. "Glad to know you're feeling better."

I was. The heady aroma of various scents – the sauces, the fresh bread, the cheese melting on the grill – mingling and overlapping each other brought back good memories of my time at Cal State. Subway, to me, has always been my go-to place whenever I wanted a pick-me-up.

"I wonder if Patricia is still working at the Subway at the campus," I mused.

He nodded. "As far as I know, she is. Why?"

"I'd like to meet her. She was good to me at a time when a lot of people in my life were not." A thought struck me with the sudden force of a lightning bolt. "Hey, do you think she might know something about Inaya? Maybe she's seen her, or has been in touch with her recently?"

Alec deliberated over it for the next couple of moments. "That might not be a bad idea. From what I remember, Inaya went to the campus Subway quite regularly after you left. If she is around, Patricia is bound to know something."

"So," I said, hurriedly stuffing the rest of the sandwich into my mouth, "what are we waiting for? Call Forrest and tell him to meet us at the campus. Let's go!"

※

"Alisha!" A voice greeted me as Alec and I entered the Subway. "You're back! Come here you!"

"I missed you, Patty," I replied. An involuntary smile made its way onto my face. Patricia's cheerful manner had made her a favourite with everyone at the campus. The extra cheese and chicken that she used to put in sandwiches didn't hurt, either.

She hung up her apron and came around the counter to give me a tight hug. "Oh, I missed you. Where have you been all this time? Are you back, for good, or are you just visiting? Would you like to have a sandwich?"

I laughed out loud. "You should have been an FBI interrogator, Patty."

"Sorry, sorry." She gave an impish smile that brought out the dimple on her left cheek. "I'm just so glad to see you."

"So am I, Patty." Once again, I couldn't help but reciprocate her impish smile. "And, to answer your questions, I've been home in India. I'm just back for a quick visit to take care of an urgent matter. And, as much as I would like to have one of your Alisha specials, I'm stuffed at the moment."

"Oh." The disappointment on her face didn't last long. She turned to Alec and Forrest with another bright smile. "And who're your companions? I remember him, though, I can't remember his name. Alex, Alan?"

"Alec. And that's Mr Forrest, our advisor," I replied. It was time to turn to the matter at hand. "Listen, Patty, we need your help."

"Anything you need, love."

"Do you remember a friend of mine? Inaya?"

Patricia shook her head. "The name seems familiar, but I can't place it with a face. Do you have a picture or something?"

I scrolled through my phone to find one of Inaya and I partying, drunk out of our minds and clicking selfies on the balcony of our apartment, and couldn't help but feel my heartache. Why did even good memories shared with people no longer in our lives hurt so much?

"Oh, I remember her!" Patricia exclaimed. "Manic Pixie Dust, or something of the sort. I have her on my Instagram account."

"You do?" I was surprised, even though I shouldn't have been. Inaya was a social butterfly – a social media butterfly. She added everybody she met to her profile.

"Yes." She took out her phone and showed it to us. Alec and Forrest leaned in to get a closer look. There was the usual smattering of Inaya's typical posts about life and chilling, from a couple of months ago. A photograph of a beautiful sunrise clicked through a steel grill and captioned 'capturing what runs free', from around 6 weeks ago. And there, unexpectedly, was her last update from three weeks ago – her location. She had been in New Jersey three weeks ago.

"What do you think?" I asked Forrest, my heart heavy with trepidation.

"I think that is what we call a lucky break," he replied. "New Jersey is worth looking into."

CRUSADING

We drove from San Bernardino to New Jersey, a cross-country adventure if there ever was one. Even with Forrest and Alec alternating between sleeping and driving, it took us the better part of two days to reach our destination. I remained curled up at the back of Forrest's station wagon, feeling so ill that I frequently threw up. By the time we reached New Jersey, all of us were not at our best humour.

To top it all, I fainted while checking in at the motel. I had hidden my aching belly from everyone.

When they rushed me to the hospital, the doctor admonished Alec and Forrest for letting me travel in my condition. Forrest was taken by surprise; Alec remained stoic.

"What in God's good name is your problem, missy?" Forrest said. I could see him struggling to keep his anger in check. "Do you want to get killed? What is this, some kind of a crusade?"

"I've told her that," Alec said without looking up from the phone. That damned thing had occupied his attention ever since I got admitted and transferred to my hospital room. Why couldn't he just let it be, for a moment?

Forrest glowered at me, nearly pink with rage. "You led me on a merry hunt when you were this close to dying yourself. You've played me for a fool."

"Mr Forrest," I replied, my voice thick with morphine. "I did not fool you. I just didn't want you to pity me because of my condition. I wanted you to help because you wanted to, not because you felt obligated to."

That seemed to cool him down a little, but not enough. "Yeah, yeah. The next time on, I want all the pertinent information up front. No missed briefs that lead to such episodes, you hear me?" He stomped back and forth for a while before going out of the room on the pretext of fetching a soda.

Alec was still busy on his phone. I wondered, for a moment, if he was playing NBA Online with Abrar again. A flash of irrational anger overpowered the calming effect of the morphine. Here he was, sitting there and playing his stupid NBA game like nothing had ever happened. My whole life had been turned upside-down and those weird sounds from the game reminded me of Abrar. I hated it.

I checked my phone and saw a text waiting for me. I immediately felt better.

```
Als, you're ignoring me like I ignore constants
in integration and semicolons in coding. Call me?
Miss you. Jay. XX
```

Without even wasting a single second I dialled his number.

"Hello? Alisha?"

I hadn't expected him to pick up the phone after just a few rings. It was a late night in India. And yet, I could hear the sound of music and revelry in the background. Jay was out, late at night. Maybe he was out on a date. That thought should not have caused me the kind of pain that it did.

"Hey, Jay," I replied. Alec finally looked up from his phone and raised an eyebrow. "Is this a good time to talk?"

There was silence on the line for a while. "Not especially, no. Is it something important?"

Was it something important? I choked back a sob. There was a time when I could have called him any time of the day or night, for anything. Nothing was ever unimportant between us. "No, nothing that important." I took a pause and then said abruptly, "I'm in the US."

That got his attention. "What?! Why?"

I hesitated for a moment, unwilling to tell him the truth. Everybody else had lectured me on why this was a misguided crusade at best. But I'd opened up to Jay once, a long time ago, and only received empathy. As much as our situation might have changed, he wouldn't have.

So I told him everything, from Inaya's email to our hunt for Abrar and Inaya, who seemed to have disappeared from the face of the earth. I also told him that I was high on morphine and irritated with Alec playing the same game he and Abrar played for hours.

"Oh, Als," he said. "I've never seen someone so foolishly brave in my entire life. Only you would risk yourself to go save someone else. Why must you be brave? You know I can't stand brave people."

A tear escaped unbidden from my eyes. "I've missed you, Jay, and I'm sorry for being so stupid back then. I just wanted someone who got me as you did. When you rejected me, everything seemed to fall apart. I reacted when I shouldn't have, I reacted how I shouldn't have."

"It's okay, Als. I understand. I've missed you, too." He paused. "You know, I've just blown off my first proper date in ages. I don't think she's calling me back."

"You'll find someone."

"Yeah, unlike you, who's having a tough time finding an ex whose possessiveness bordered on human rights violation."

I laughed. And just like that, the petty grudges melted like ice on a hot summer day. "Don't joke about this. It's a serious matter."

"With you, my dude, what isn't?" He replied. "What's the hang-up with finding Abrar, anyway?"

"We are trying." Alec continued playing the stupid game, mixing its weird sounds with the beeping monitors. "Alec stop it or I'll kill you, I swear."

"Abrar used to play an online game? I can track his IP Address."

"You can do that?" I sat up straight in surprise. Alec was by my side in a moment, worried I might fall off the bed.

"You can't? I thought you had a police detective helping you."

"Forrest, yes, but we didn't mention the game. What do you need to track him down?"

"Just the name of the game and his user ID, and a couple of hours. Do you have those?"

I covered the mouthpiece. "What was Abrar's username on NBA Online?"

"Lucifer663," Alec replied. I passed on the information to Jay. "What's this about, Alisha?"

I looked at Alec's puzzled face and mouthed, *I'll explain it later.* "Alright, I am counting on you, Jay."

"Anytime, Als. Wait for my message."

The next couple of hours passed fitfully. Forrest had come back from his excursion and we updated him on everything that had happened. Though initially surprised, the ex-detective had responded with a cool impassiveness that suggested he didn't want to count his chickens before they hatched. With the morphine kicking in, I drifted in and out of restless sleep. Alec had been given the responsibility to wake me up if Jay called or texted.

Finally, some four hours after we spoke, I received a single message:

234, YELLOW PINE TOWN.

"Yellow Pine?" Forrest looked shocked. "That can't be right."

"Why?" I asked.

"Because, missy, it's one of the few backwater places left in America. Can you imagine a town spread across almost 200 square miles with a population of less than 100? It's a place that doesn't want to change. It doesn't want modern gadgets or technology. I'm sure there is inbreeding and stuff as well. Otherwise, it would be hard to explain how the town survives, even though no one ever visits," he replied, shaking his head. "Yellow Pine, huh. The bastard's got some nerve."

This time it was Alec who questioned him. "Why?"

"It is an unincorporated settlement. It means there is no municipal government, no local law officials. Everything is done at the county level, and I doubt anyone of them wants to go down to that particular hellhole for anything. Not that those creepy bastards would ever raise an alarm if anything went amiss. It's spooky as hell, the kind of town that horror movies are based in. Your quarry has chosen his nest well."

"Not well enough. If it's a small settlement, they should be easy to find," I said. "Go, get that bastard. Make him pay for what he's done."

LOSING HOPE

Hey, hope I helped A text from Jay flashed on my phone.

Yes, the boys are on their way to Yellow Pine.

And where are you?

Chilling in the bathtub of a five-star suite with champagne and oysters. I replied, taking a break from using the words 'uselessly dying in the hospital'

Morose humour. You seem to be in a good mood today. I'm calling.

The phone rang the next instant. The boy did not waste any time getting shit done.
  "Yo, what's up?" Jay said. His inordinate cheerful mood was the farthest cry from how I felt.
  "Nothing much, just timing the vitals monitor to see if it beeps exactly after 1.5 seconds. It's faltered seven times since the morning, which makes me wonder whether it will work if my vitals start dropping."

"That restless?"

"Yes, and nervous," I confessed. "I didn't expect to be strapped to all these machines and drips while others went after Abrar. I can only hope they find him. We have no leads after this. It was good luck enough that I caught up with you when I did."

"Yes, my saviour. Oh, if it weren't for you, who would have broken my fall?"

I rolled my eyes. "Jay, that wasn't funny. At all."

"I know. I realised it as soon as I said it. Sounded funnier in my head."

"Everything sounds funnier in your head," I replied. "You should try not blurting the first thing that comes to your mind, sometime."

"Maybe I will."

There was a sound at the door. Was it a knock? The doorknob moved. The door opened and, standing there, tall and dark and menacing as I last remembered him, was Abrar.

"Hello, Alisha," he said.

I froze. What was Abrar doing at the hospital? How did he find me here? Where was Inaya? So many questions clanged around my brain like debris in a tornado.

"Some people at the campus heard you were looking for Inaya and were coming to New Jersey. The rest was a matter of perseverance. One thing led to another, and it wasn't that tough to track you to the hospital." He smiled as he sat down on the only chair in the room. Once upon a time, I would have found it disarming. Now, it felt wolfish, sinister. "Relax, Alisha. I am not here to hurt you. I am happy to see you, feisty you."

"What *are* you here for, Abrar?" I asked, trying to keep the quaver out of my voice. "And where is Inaya?"

"Inaya is not your concern," he replied. "She's fine wherever she is."

"Fine like I was, Abrar, when you locked me up in the bathroom for two days without food, water, or clothes, for daring to say no to you? Or fine like when you beat me up so bad for talking to a guy who won't give up pursuing me against my wishes? Or fine like so many other times when you either bullied me, beat me up, or drugged me? Is that the baseline we're operating with?"

His expression darker than the night sky on a moonless night, Abrar leaned forward in his seat. For a moment, I thought that he would hit me again.

"Do you ever listen to yourself, Alisha? Me, me, me, me, me – that's all you talk about. Your issues, your trauma. Did you ever think about what I've gone through, what I continue to go through? The demons that plague me?"

It was a classic misdirection. Once again, Abrar wanted to shift the blame to his issues, taking no accountability for his actions.

But, this time, I did not bend to his will. Fury made me see things clearer. I was facing the monster who had broken me into a million pieces. Now those little pieces were an army of me which hated him with a million times passion. He could not break me further.

"For how long will you give the same excuses, Abrar? For how long will you continue to blame your past for your present, for your future? For how long will you hold others responsible for your actions?" I shouted. "You took advantage of me because I was openly vulnerable around you. But why did you target Inaya? Why did you destroy an innocent girl like that?"

"Because that's the only thing that makes me feel alive," Abrar whispered. "Do you want to know why I did what I did to you? Why do I have Inaya with me right now? My demons demand sacrifice all the time. Every moment of every day, they want their pound of soul. They consume me if I don't constantly feed them. They torture me, make me see life through things I would much rather have buried in the past. The only way to escape that agony is to find someone else to be the object of their malice. It was nothing personal, Alisha. You, Inaya, everyone I've been with – they're all just walls that protect me from my demons."

I was beyond horrified; I also sought vengeance. My stars must have been in some especially lucky alignment that I ever escaped Abrar's clutches. This broken, twisted person could pass off as a functioning human being most of the time. He used his charms on me before hurting me – and now he was doing the same thing with my friend.

Cold rage gripped me. "Where is Inaya, Abrar? Where have you kept her?"

He looked at me, then, as if seeing me for the first time. "Why did you go to the cops, Alisha? Why are you doing this to me? Don't you love me?"

"I have never loved you! You're sick, Abrar, and your madness is dangerous to those around you. You took everything away from me – my self-respect, my sense of worth, my happiness. Now you're doing the same with my friend. I will not let you break Inaya the way you broke me. You gave me nothing but shame." Words escaped me with the force of a raging tsunami. "I will reclaim myself. I will make myself whole again. I will make you pay for your crimes Abrar, even if it's the last thing I do on this earth."

"And what if she's already broken? What if whatever you're doing is pointless? What if there's no saving Inaya, no redemption waiting for you at the end of the tunnel?" The glint in his eye made my hackles rise. "Why would you want to jump into a river that you know is going to drown you? I like you, Alisha. I want you to stay away from all this."

"You know, it's a curious thing. You blame me but never reflect upon your actions. You don't see how you have created this situation that you find so abhorrent," he continued. "Inaya wouldn't be in this position if it wasn't for you. If you hadn't involved her, if you hadn't left, she wouldn't be with me. With you, I could have gotten better. Inaya is just reckless. You made your choice, she made hers. And now you both have to live with them."

Anger suffused my being, filled every nerve, every muscle with fire. I wanted to hit Abrar with the first thing I could get my hands on. My fingers brushed against my phone. As I moved to pick it up, I saw there was an ongoing call. Jay had heard everything we had talked about.

"Not reckless, Abrar, she is innocent. Please let her go!"

"You should leave us alone, Alisha. What is done is done. This little adventure needs to end, now, or someone will get hurt real bad. Forget Inaya and go home. You don't want to get on my bad side. Take care of yourself." Abrar got up from his seat and kissed me on my forehead. "Goodbye, Alisha."

I was struggling to move while he did that. I wanted to smack him with all my strength, but my body was paralyzed with overwhelming fear.

It took me a while to realise that he had dismissed me from his audience. He was here, without my permission, making me revisit the scars of the past. Now he was leaving without receiving any of the retribution due upon him. It galled me to see him escape scot-free, once again.

"You're not going anywhere, Abrar," I shouted, struggling with the thousand and one contraptions that bound me to the bed and the medical system. "Stop right there!"

He turned around at the door and gave me that wolfish grin once again. "Try to make me." And with that, he was gone.

I ran after him, as best as I could. The haze of morphine dragged me down. One of the needles stuck to me had come loose when I left the bed. Bright red blood now flowed from the puncture, dripping down my hand, onto my phone, and on the tiled flooring below. The patients and visitors I passed gave me inquiring glances but didn't say a word; the situation was too strange for them to intervene. They didn't want to be wrapped up in someone else's nightmare.

I burst through the outer door of the building, only to see Abrar getting into a bright red Dodge Coronet convertible and backing out of the parking. I ran after him and, for a moment, I thought he would run me over. He swerved at the last moment. I staggered from the glancing blow and, recovering, picked up a rock and threw it in his direction with all the strength I could muster. It struck the tail-light, which shattered before the car drove away.

He was gone.

He was gone.

He was gone.

There is no death worse than the end of hope, it is said. At that moment, I felt the weight of that truth. Hope had been the engine that kept me going, despite the challenges, despite my physical frailty. I had staked my chances of making peace with myself on that one forlorn hope of bringing Abrar to justice and getting some closure. As it vanished in front of my eyes in the dust thrown up by his car, the emotional baggage I carried - the traumas, the scars, the memories - never felt so heavy.

Despite everything I'd done, he had won again. I fell to my knees and cried endlessly. I had lost.

WE'LL BE FINE

"It's no use, Mr Forrest," I replied. "He's gone. There's no one here anymore. Let's call off this thing and go back."

On the other end of the phone, Forrest and Alec were saying something. I wasn't listening. Jay had called them up after Abrar's unexpected visit, making them turn back to the hospital. Forrest had called in his favours within the police force and was preparing to get a security detail assigned to me – which was about as useful as bandaging a decapitated head.

"I'm tired, Mr Forrest," I said, truthfully. "I'll talk to you when you're here."

The phone rang within a minute of disconnecting. I suppressed my irritation. As sweet as the gesture was, the two of them needed to understand that I did not need their attention right now. Fully intending to let loose the day's frustration, I picked up the call.

And stopped. The person on the other line was neither Alec nor Forrest. It was my sister.

"Hey," Akira said. "How are you?"

For a moment, I wanted to tell her to go away. I'd had a bad day, and I didn't want to let in my good-for-nothing, selfish sister on the fact that I was dying on a hospital bed in New Jersey.

I took a deep breath and suppressed my irritation. "Hey, Akira," I replied. "I'm well. How are things over at your end?"

"They're good. They're good. Rohit is busy planning our next getaway. He says we need a break. He's been working way too hard, and my office has been kind of crazy, lately." There was a brief pause. "You know, Alisha, I spoke with dad yesterday."

"That's great," I said. So that's why she called. Dad must have guilt-tripped her into speaking with me. He was always the glue that held our dysfunctional family together. "I haven't been able to get a chance to call. I've been very busy recently."

"Yeah, I heard what you're doing." Another pause. "Tell me more. How's it going?"

This was strange. Akira rarely called and, when she did, her conversations were all about her – what she was doing, what she was planning to do, what had happened to her. To say my issues took a backseat would be an overstatement; we *never* discussed me.

"Akira." I was in no mood for games. "Is everything okay?"

"Yes," she replied, almost too quickly. "No, everything isn't okay, Alisha. You're there, all alone, doing what you're doing. Here I am, with no clue about the danger that my sister is heading into. It's always been this way. I've been an awful sibling, haven't I?"

I bit back the retort and chose silence instead. After a while, she continued. "For what it's worth, I just want to tell you that I'm sorry. I'm sorry that I haven't been there for you more. I wish I could roll back time and be more considerate. But, while we can't change what happened now, I'm proud of what you're doing. I would have never been able to do that. I want to be as strong as you are, Alisha, and I won't hesitate to admit that you've become my role model. Go, be a champ, sister, like you've always been."

The sudden outpour caught me off-guard. What had just happened? Was my sister warming up to me, after all these years? "Akira, I don't..."

"I hope Alec is there. I trust he will take good care of you. I am sorry, Alisha. I really am. I have been nothing but a coward. I love you." She laughed. "Woah, It feels good to say that." I had liked the sound of her laughter since childhood. I couldn't remember the last time I had heard her laugh so freely.

"Yes, it does," I replied.

"Meet me soon. Do you want me there?"

"I am fine, Akira. All of this means so much to me, I am sorry if I have ever hurt you," I confessed with tearful eyes.

"Make us proud."

"I think I am losing. I don't think I'll be able to do that," I was crying like a baby.

"Aalu, you are a freaking warrior. Nothing can defeat you. Use your skills, use your strength. We are all with you!"

I gazed at the far wall for a long time after the call disconnected. Seconds trickled into minutes, minutes turned into hours. I couldn't believe that things were finally turning around for me. The rekindling of my friendship with Alec and Jay, Forrest's compassion and willingness, Patricia's warmth, the heart-to-heart call with Akira – all of these things were beginning to fill a void inside of me that had existed for as long as I could remember. I had a family. I had love. I had friends.

I had hope – and with hope came action. I dialled up Forrest's number.

"Alisha?" Alec picked up the phone. "Are you okay? Are you safe?"

"I'm okay," I said and meant it. "Alec, could you put Forrest on the line?"

There was some shuffling, the sound of phone changing hands, and Forrest's gruff voice came through. "Listen, missy, you stay put where you are. We're coming, and so are the detectives."

"Yeah, you might want to hold onto that thought," I said. Could it work? Could what I was thinking work? There was only one way to know. "When Abrar visited, I caught a glimpse of his car. It was a bright red Dodge Coronet. A convertible Dodge Coronet."

"A Dodge Coronet?" I could sense the change in Forrest's tone. He was excited – just as I had hoped he would be. "Not many of those around anymore. Not in this area, and definitely not convertibles."

"And fewer still with a broken tail-light." I narrated the entire incident to them, of how I chased after Abrar and threw a rock at his car, breaking one of his tail-lights.

"I'll get the New Jersey PD to put out an APB-BOL." Forrest was silent for a moment, before continuing like a proud guardian to their ward. "That's some good detective work there, missy. I'll keep you posted if we get a hit."

"Forrest," I said with a broken voice. "We still don't have any evidence."

I could hear light laughter.

"Jay had called me much earlier when he heard Abrar with you. He has recorded your conversation, we have all the evidence we need. God bless androids."

※

One would imagine that the hours after my call with Forrest would be nerve-racking and full of tension. They were the opposite. I slept like a baby knowing what Jay had done for me. The excitement of the day, combined with my health and the morphine, had completely worn me out. When I finally woke up, there were five missed calls – two from Alec, two from Forrest, and one from Jay.

I called up Alec first. "Inaya, we found her!" he blurted as soon as the call connected. "But the bastard managed to escape. He was staying with her at a small motel on the outskirts of New Jersey. The car was here. He had reached the motel but seemed like he had discovered we were on his trail. He fled."

"Is Inaya okay? What's the address?" I asked.

"What?" He said. "Oh, no. No, no, no, no, no. You're not coming, Alisha, not in the condition you're in."

"Please, Alec." I wanted to see this through to the end. I wanted Abrar to know that I was the one who brought him to justice. But now that he had fled, I wanted to be as close to justice as possible; with Inaya. "I have to. Please, just tell me where she is. I'll be fine, I promise."

I could tell that he was reluctant to share the information, but something in my tone – the burning need, perhaps, for closure – made him change his mind. "Alright, fine."

I noted the address down on a piece of paper and rang up the reception to begin my check-out. The doctor resisted, as I knew he would, but I was not ready to take no for an answer. Not anymore.

The drive took an hour, a long hour in which I ran over many scenarios in my head while I sobbed over our victory. What would I say to Inaya? How would she be, emotionally, mentally? What if what Abrar had said was true? What if it was already too late?

My hour of agonising thoughts finally came to an end when the cab stopped at the destination. I got out and paid the fare. There were several police vehicles around the motel, creating a protective cordon. I searched for familiar faces – Alec, Inaya, Forrest – to get my bearings.

A dark-skinned police officer barred my way. "Active crime scene, miss. For your safety, I'd advise you to stay at a distance."

"It's okay," Forrest called out. "She's with me."

After we walked past the vehicles and towards the motel, Forrest turned to me. "Dear God, missy, you were right. In all my years of service, I've never seen such a twisted crime scene."

"What do you mean by crime scene?" My heart skipped a beat. "What happened? Is Inaya okay?"

"Depends on what you mean by okay. Apart from a few cuts and bruises here and there, and some old scars, she's fine. But she's not all *there*, right now, if you get what I mean. The paramedics will treat her physical bruises, but the emotional ones..." He looked around apprehensively. "They might take a long time."

"Take me to her."

"The medics are still checking up on her but in the meantime, there's something you should see. Come with me." He led me to the Dodge and I followed his gaze to a note lying on the driver's seat. "I'll give you some space," he distanced away, but not too far.

I know you won't give up so I'll give you what you want. She's inside. I've been caving into my demons all my life and I'll pay for my sins on my account when the time comes. But for now, I'm letting this go and it's better if you do the same. You got what you wanted, now give me what I deserve. A second chance. You fought your demons. Now give me a chance to fight mine. Let me go, Alisha. Don't come after me. Abrar.

I read and reread the note. Forrest came up to my side and placed a hand on my shoulder.

"Inaya's here. As for the fucker, he couldn't have gone much far. We'll get him. Don't worry."

Worry, my ass. At that moment, I only had eyes for Inaya.

She was sitting on a stretcher, with a couple of towels and a curtain draped over her. Alec was kneeling next to her, stroking her head soothingly, trying to coax a reaction out of her inert frame. He looked relieved when he saw me.

"I'm sorry, Alisha." He looked sheepish. "We've tried everything. She doesn't respond."

Upon hearing my name, Inaya raised her head and looked at me. With a guttural cry, she crawled forward, put her arms around my legs, and started to cry. It was a déjà vu moment, the same way I had crawled to her when she had saved me 2 years ago.

"I'm sorry, Ali," she said between deep, heaving sobs which racked her fragile frame. "I'm so sorry for everything."

I knelt next to my friend, my mind drifting back to a scene that had occurred a long time ago, in a place not that far away. I remembered everything that had happened since and smiled.

"She will be okay. She'll be fine. I'll take her with me," I said as I took her hand in mine and gave it a little squeeze. "I know she will learn to be fine."

EPILOGUE

As Inaya and I recovered together at the hospital, Alec took care of us. I wondered why he did so much? Do people do this for each other or was he different? Alec had never asked me for anything and we had never shared our deepest thoughts, then why were we inseparable this way? What had intrigued us about each other? I could only ever wonder.

He approached me with a latte, two sugars. "Alec, why did you risk your life for me?"

"That's what friends are for," he shrugged.

"I don't think I'll ever be able to reciprocate"

"God forbid, I'll ever have to hunt down my abuser, girl. God forbid!" We both laughed.

He dropped us off at the airport. Inaya hardly said anything the whole way. Her family had not answered any of her calls yet.

"Bye Inaya. Just remember, if you let what happened overpower you, you have the biggest example here. Conquer it," Alec said to Inaya as he pointed towards me.

"I had you. Alec. She has me," I looked at Inaya assuringly and smiled.

"Thank you for saving our life, Alec. Again." I hugged him as I handed over my black necklace to him which he had given to Jay. "It belongs only to you. I love you bro."

Inaya and I sat on a plane bound for India. Her ordeal had left her exhausted and she was sleeping with her head resting on my shoulder. I looked at her and remembered how relieved I'd felt, two years ago; to be going back home, eager to put the nightmare I had survived behind me. I'd slept through most of the flight, knowing that I was finally safe. I wondered if she felt the same way, if she'd need to recuperate the way I did. Or maybe she would find a different path to healing.

Regardless, she could always do with a little nudge. I asked the hostess for a notepad and a pen.

Dear Inaya, I wrote.

I wish I knew how to begin this letter. Shared trauma binds us, and so does betrayal, love and friendship. How do you even start a letter that contains all of that?

I tapped the notepad with the pen. I'd barely started, and I was already stuck. What did I want to say to her?

What happened to you – to us – was unimaginably monstrous. No one ever thinks they'd have to face something like that. And yet we did. The nightmare enveloped us, consumed us, unravelled our innermost selves and broke us into a million pieces. But it's over now, and the question that remains in front of us is: what now? The answer is easy. We need to heal. Saying that is easy. Achieving it can be daunting.

I should know. My road to healing was full of hardships. I learned, through the painful process of trial and error; progress on this path is never linear. *Sometimes you may take one* step forward, only to take two steps back. Sometimes you wander down a narrow side-road that seems like a shortcut, only to double back. Sometimes you get so frustrated that you want to give up completely and let your demons consume you. What's the worst that could happen, you feel after all that has already happened?

Giving up – that's the worst thing that could happen. Abrar couldn't see a beautiful, free thing like you flourish because he felt incapable of ever being as free, as beautiful as you are. So he chose the coward's way. He decided to bring you down to your level by crushing your spirit. If you give up, you will let your trauma and your tormentor win. I know it will be hard to keep going, at times. I've felt that same urge that you'll feel, from time to time, to just let everything implode. Don't give into it. Break your progress into smaller and smaller parts, into small battles that you can fight and win. Go halfway and just a step further, so that it takes more effort to come back than it takes to keep moving forward. Don't worry, you will have plenty of help. You'll find all your broken pieces, every single one of them, along this hard but fruitful journey.

As you continue to move forward, collect them all and hold them close to your chest. They are your army. Where there was one, now there will be many. Most importantly, they belonged to the person that you were – and they will belong to the person that you will be, once more. Then there's me. I'll be here, my friend, to help you as my friends helped me. I'll be here to listen to you, to guide you on your journey, to pick you up when you're feeling low. I will do this because I love you, and I forgive you. People will tell you that you are broken. But you will not always remain that way. You will learn to heal, Ina, and you'll learn to put yourself back together. The scars will remain, they always remain; the reminders of a past that you'd much rather forget. But you will learn to master the pain. It will gradually hurt lesser and lesser until, one day, it will be no more than a dull ache. You will learn to be strong for yourself. I know it, friend. In time, you will. Always remember - To be born, to love and to die are the three most crucial parts of our lives, the rest are just reactions to that."

I folded the piece of paper and slipped it into her jacket as she slept.

Hey Jay, we won.

I typed on my phone.

We're coming back. Remember how you once said that everyone is broken, but others don't need to bleed on their edges? I think I understand that now. And I know that I love you. I'll see you soon.

Before I hit send, I deleted the penultimate line. Some things don't need to be said, and some things shouldn't be said. It would find its way out, when the time would be right. Likewise, I had so much to say to Alec too. Some other time maybe. I smiled, closed my eyes, and settled in.
    I was going back home.
    Again.

www.ingramcontent.com/pod-product-compliance
Lightning Source LLC
LaVergne TN
LVHW041707060526
838201LV00043B/616